THE DOM NEXT DOOR

A BAD BOY BILLIONAIRE ROMANCE

MICHELLE LOVE

CONTENTS

	Sign Up to Receive Free Books	1
	Synopsis	3
1.	Emmeline	5
2.	Carl	17
3.	Emmeline	23
4.	Carl	29
5.	Emmeline	40
6.	Carl	48
7.	Emmeline	54
8.	Carl	60
9.	Emmeline	65
10.	Carl	72
11.	Emmeline	79
	Sign Up to Receive Free Books	86

Made in "The United States" by:

Michelle Love

© Copyright 2020 – Michelle Love

ISBN: 978-1-64808-240-5

ALL RIGHTS RESERVED. No part of this publication may be reproduced or transmitted in any form whatsoever, electronic, or mechanical, including photocopying, recording, or by any informational storage or retrieval system without express written, dated and signed permission from the author

✿ Created with Vellum

SIGN UP TO RECEIVE FREE BOOKS

Sign Up to Receive Free E-Books and Audiobook Codes.

Would you like to read **Savage Hearts** and **other romance books** for **free**?

You can sign up to receive free e-books and audiobooks by typing this link into your browser:

https://ivywondersauthor.com/ivy-wonders-author

SYNOPSIS

Shy, lonely Emmeline grew up in an upper class New Orleans Creole family in a dim, cool antebellum mansion with endless rooms. Bullied by her strange, nasty older sister, Shayla, she became quiet and introspective, relying on her faith to sustain her. Her path was clear, and she'd decided that she would become a novitiate nun after completing junior college. But everything changed when her parents were brutally murdered, and though she escaped with her life, she lost her faith.

Now, driven out of her childhood home by her sister, the young heiress has settled into her first new house and is trying to put her life back together. The one bright spot in her life is the hunky single dad who lives in the mansion next door. Carl makes her feel things she's never felt before, even with a simple look her way.

Widower and single dad Carl made his billions in the legal cannabis market—but he made his seed money in the years before, flying Jamaican gold over the border to sell to smoke-hungry Americans. A Dom by nature, he's strongly attracted to demure young Emmeline...and is more than happy to make the first move when he realizes that she is too shy to do so herself.

But even as they finally start to get to know each other, Shayla's planning her next move. She wants Emmeline's share of the inheritance, she wants her new house, and she's determined to get them both. Soon the new lovers find themselves fighting against the same psychopath who murdered Emmeline's parents —on Shayla's orders.

Blurb

I used to know exactly what I would do with my life, and why. I planned to devote myself to God. I was in the middle of my novice training a little over a year ago, when someone blew up my parents' car. They were the kindest people in the world, and their deaths shook the foundation of my faith.

Now I'm lost, knocking around in a half-furnished new house with no family left but a sister who hates me. No one has ever found the people responsible for my parents' murder, and the police don't seem interested in trying to find them, either. The only bright spot in my life is the man who lives next door with his baby daughter.

I look at him and remember that I'm a woman, not just a failed novice. He gives me one smile, and I feel some of the glacier of grief inside of me melt away.

I can only imagine what a kiss from him would do.

1
EMMELINE

"Hi, Mom. Hi, Dad. Sorry I haven't visited in a while."

My coat is too thin for this weather. The chilly breeze blows across the hillside and rustles the flattened dead grass before cutting through the wool. It's the only black coat I have, however, and I've been using it exclusively for a year, for just that reason.

Mom and Dad had insisted in their living will on a burial on the same low hill where our ancestors' graves have sat for centuries. The small mausoleum, a plain filing box for two coffins, sits before me as I crouch down with the icy wind at my back.

"It's snowing again. Second time this winter. It's crazy. Cars are piling up on the highways, and over in Florida the iguanas are falling out of trees from the cold. Can you imagine?"

My laugh is small, awkward and hollow, and the wind carries it away quickly.

This doesn't feel like New Orleans. There shouldn't be snow here. This winter feels wrong.

But things have felt wrong for months now. None of it makes sense—but I'm not all that surprised. My whole world has felt crazy ever since my parents died.

"I'm not going to the convent after all. I know, I said I was doing that right after junior college, but I'm realizing more and more that after what happened to you, my faith…just didn't end up being my rock like I thought it was."

My voice breaks and I go silent, cold tears tracking down my cheeks. The Mother Superior of the convent I had been seeking membership with was very sympathetic, but she didn't understand. But she'd also never seen her parents blown up right in front of her.

Seen? No, felt—my whole vision had been whited out by the fireball. One moment, I was walking to the car, my Dad talking to me from the driver's side, teasing me gently for forgetting my phone while my mother hid a smile. The next, a tremendous blast of heat hit me and hurtled me backward, my own awkward smile barely having time to die before I landed in our hedge. After that, everything went black.

I SPENT last January in the hospital, first for burns and cracked ribs, and then for post-traumatic stress. They released me with a clean bill of health, but they were dead wrong.

MOM AND DAD have been in their grave a year, and I haven't felt right or healthy in all that time. I can function day to day now—I can manage my money, and I have my own house. But part of me died that day with my parents—I woke up in the hospital without it, and haven't been able to find it since.

"I'M SORRY, Mom. I know you were proud when I decided to devote myself to God. But I can't join a religious order without faith."

THE FAITH that had sustained me since I was six years old, which I had turned to over and over again when my sister Shayla wreaked havoc in my life, crumbled like sand in the face of that explosion. The arsonist hasn't been caught, Shayla is three times worse without my parents' disapproval to restrain her, and every comforting word from a priest or the Bible...no longer comforts.

THE TEARS WON'T STOP. In the time since my parents have been gone, I've slowly been able to cut down on the public sobbing fits, hating to embarrass myself like that. But right now, I can forgive myself for breaking down a little.

. . .

"I'm going back to college. I'll finish my degree and then...well...I'm not sure. But I'll try to find some way to make you proud of me." *I hope.*

Lucky for me that my half of the inheritance will carry me my whole life—even if I were never able to handle a job again.

"I still can't get along with Shayla," I mumble, wiping my cheeks again. "She pushed me into leaving home. I could only turn the other cheek so many times, so I left. I'm sure she planned it that way.

"I think you would like my new house, though. It's not very big, but it's well-restored, it's clean, and it's mine. The neighborhood isn't as nice as ours, but...one of the neighbors...well, he's *very* nice."

The thought of Carl, the single dad next door, makes me smile enough that my tears dry for a while. I can't even fully explain how much the thought of him comforts me. Watching him play with his cute little daughter, his huge, powerful form moving so gently around her, always makes me happy.

Then there are the dreams I have about him...but I'm not going to go dwelling on *them* in front of my parents' grave. Still, I giggle a little. "I think you would like him."

. . .

"Like who?" snaps a voice behind me, and I freeze. The voice is a little distant, and I hear the shuffle of feet coming up through the dead grass. *Shayla.* I shudder and clench my fists to calm myself, glad at least that she wasn't standing behind me listening the whole time I was lost in my talk with the dead.

"None of your business," I say as firmly as I can, cursing the tiny shake I can hear in my voice as she stalks around me and dumps an enormous bouquet atop the mausoleum. Purple monkshood clashes gaudily with orange lilies, hot pink snapdragons, and blood-colored rhododendron, crowding out my simple garland of white roses.

"I can't believe you're up here talking to a couple of corpses in a marble box. They're fucking dead, you melodramatic twit. Life after death is a myth, just like your god."

I hold myself very still, the anger and resentment I've felt for as long as I can remember burning inside of me like an ember. I won't give her the satisfaction of breaking down in front of her, or of losing my temper. Either reaction will leave that narcissistic cow thinking she's in control.

"Emmeline, can you hear me or did your shrink put you on more tranquilizers?" Her voice is a mocking whine as she turns to confront me.

. . .

I STRAIGHTEN, lifting my head, and meet her sharp, dark gaze with my own. My sister looks older and crueler every time I see her. Her mouth is a narrow, dry slit thinly lined in dark red, her eyes are sunken and hold a greedy gleam, and her straight, russet-bronze hair—so like my own—has been clipped to her jawline and streaked with gold.

SHE WEARS a silk suit the exact color of her lipstick with no blouse underneath, her silicone-enhanced cleavage tastelessly exposed. On the whole, she's wearing too much musky perfume and too much gold, too many jewels, and not one single indication of grief or loss. That's my big sister: making wealthy, slutty sociopathy fashionable again.

SHE SEEMS ABSOLUTELY stunned by my mute, expressionless examination of her. She doesn't understand just how done with her I am. She never has been able to understand boundaries; even when my father would shout at her at the top of his lungs for her latest round of household thefts, she'd always claim he was "overreacting." She's immune from guilt.

BUT SHE'S ABSOLUTELY unused to my standing up to her.

"SHAYLA, I've put up with a lot of your shit over the years, but I refuse to do it at our parents' grave. Knock it off, or we're done for good."

SHE'S BLINKING VERY RAPIDLY NOW, her vain, narrow little mind struggling to process where my show of backbone came from. The thing is, I always had a backbone; I just wasn't confrontational. I was shy and kind instead.

INSTEAD OF PUNCHING my sister in the face when she stole my clothes and ruined them, or was cruel to me at school, I turned the other cheek, and prayed, and felt better. I listened to my apologetic parents trying to explain to me that *Shayla is sick*, that *she can't help herself*, and that I had to be strong. I did as they asked, for the sake of family harmony.

BUT THEN MY PARENTS' car exploded with them in it, and me just steps away from joining them. If I hadn't gone back for my phone, I would have died with them.

SHAYLA DIDN'T VISIT me in the hospital. She greeted me without warmth or sympathy when I returned. Instead, upon hearing that I wasn't going to join a convent like I had planned, she drove me out of our family home, claiming it for herself.

HER WAYS of driving me out had been very effective, making sure that I couldn't stay no matter how much I wanted to. Banging on my door at all hours of the night. Breaking into my room. Stealing and breaking my things. Screaming at me and lecturing me every day, sometimes for hours.

I LEFT AS SOON as I could gather enough of my inheritance together to pay for my new home in cash. That was months ago, and the venom still hasn't left my veins. Instead, it's killed my ability to give a single damn about being nice to Shayla.

"I can't believe you! How rude can you be? Telling me to shut up! I'm only saying these things for your own good—"

"You came into this conversation being the biggest bitch you could be, and now you're hurt that I'm not happy to see you?" I snort, tucking a few strands of hair behind my ear that have escaped my braid. "Drop the act. Nobody's ever happy to see you, Shayla, because you're a soulless bitch."

"When in the Hell did the aspiring nun take up swearing?" She finally manages to mumble. She sounds incredulous, as if I've suddenly sprouted a pair of devil horns.

"I'm not an aspiring nun anymore," I growl, scooping up my shoulder bag and turning to go.

"Wait, wait! We have to talk about finances!" She starts to move to intercept me, but I step quickly away from her and stalk off down the hill. My Doc Martens have better purchase on the slippery hillside than her stiletto heels, and I hear her yelp with dismay as she falls behind. "Come back here, you rude little bitch!"

I'm cold all over by the time I reach my pickup, but I refuse to let the tears fall. My grief curdles my stomach, but I won't take even the slightest chance that Shayla might catch me crying. If she finds me in tears, she will laugh.

THROUGH THE RAGE, I feel an unexpected surge of pride in how I'm handling this. *I actually stood up to her.* It was bitter, mean, and clumsy, but I did it.

I DON'T EVEN LET myself wonder why she's trying to talk to me about money—except, of course, that it's the thing she loves best in the world. Maybe she's after my half of the inheritance. She's always been jealous of anything my parents gave me—including life.

WHEN I WAS little I used to try so hard to get Shayla to like me. I used to cry with frustration over it, and that would make her laugh with delight at how hard I was trying, even though I always failed.

NOW, as I drive home in uncharacteristically thin New Orleans traffic, I think to myself that the only effort she'll be getting from me from now on is the bare minimum it takes to keep me from beating her physically and landing in jail. A tiny, heartbroken part of me, the part who realizes that Shayla is the only family I have left in the world now that Mom and Dad are gone, knows that I should hurt unbearably. But instead, the whole encounter has just left me very, very tired.

. . .

When I pull up in front of the stately white home with its double wraparound porches and iron railings, I have to take a breath for a moment before pulling into the driveway. But the tall iron gates open automatically at my truck's approach, and I drive inside unchallenged.

Once I've parked the truck in the open carport, I walk inside...and feel a wave of relief wash over me. *Alone.* Alone in my own home, which I bought with my own money, in a safe neighborhood far from my sister.

How wonderful to not have to share a space with her after those months of psychological warfare. Maybe, next time I see her, I should say goodbye for good, and lift the weight of knowing her from my heart forever. It won't make up for my losses, but it will sure make my life easier.

She's petty and cruel to me. She never shed a single tear over our parents. There's nothing there to miss.

The house is mostly barren inside: the only parts that I have fully furnished so far are the kitchen, one bathroom, and the master bedroom. I pass by a living room that is still piled with boxes I just haven't opened yet. Moving had exhausted me, like so much else does these days. Now, I just make myself unpack and set up a few things a day, and stop when I start to get weepy or sick.

. . .

THE ENCOUNTER with Shayla has left me even more drained than usual, to the point where I can feel myself shaking slightly. I decide on a nap. My therapist has worked hard to get me to look after myself better, especially when I start showing warning signs of a meltdown. Apparently some of it has sunk in.

MY BEDROOM IS EXACTLY as I had dreamed it would look back when I was a little girl and couldn't have any elegant things thanks to my sister. The enormous white iron canopy bed, with its frame draped in fairy lights and multicolored gauze, the patchwork velvet coverlet in copper and green, the Susan Seldon Boulet prints of unicorns and women, hanging on the white plaster walls, all of them new and undamaged. It's a haven for me—one I'm grateful to have after the trials of the last year.

IN THE AFTERNOONS when I take my naps, I fall asleep to birdsong. In the mornings, when I can sleep as long as I need without being shouted at, I wake up to the same songs. And sometimes I also hear a deep voice calling happily, and a little girl giggling–and that is the best thing around here to wake up to.

CARL. The grizzled mystery man next door, who loves his daughter and fills her days with laughter and joy. He's huge compared to me, all muscle, with shaggy blond hair, narrow blue eyes and a smile like the sun coming up. I can pretty much remember the exact moment that I fell in love with him.

I WAS DIRECTING the small group of gardeners I'd hired to tame the then jungle in my backyard when I saw him playing with his daughter for the first time. I didn't mean to spy on them, exactly–I never do–but on that day, I was captivated. As I watched him being so kind and gentle with the girl, I wondered: would he be just as kind and tender with the woman he loves as well?

The dreams of him had started almost right away. I welcome them, because they drown out the nightmares. I would rather wake up shivering in the middle of the night with unfamiliar pleasure and need than with terror and loss. Those dreams—those feelings—are like an invitation away from despair and back to life.

This time, I don't dream of anything at all. But I smile—really smile, for the first time that day—when that now familiar sound wakes me up. It's that lovely deep voice again, singing a few bits of a kids' song while his little girl giggles louder and louder.

Spirits lifting, I head to my window to watch.

2

CARL

The cute little lady next door is watching us again. She's harmless, so I don't mind. I get the impression that she's shy and awkward, more than anything. Skittish, like a stray kitten.

My guess is she's recovering from something. Her shyness, her listlessness, her lack of visitors—they all point to someone who has withdrawn to lick her wounds. She seems like someone who needs to be taken care of. And when I look at her...I think that I really wouldn't mind volunteering.

She's adorable. Statuesque and sexy, but demure, with wide, dark eyes I could fall into, and a gorgeous mane of auburn hair she braids and ties up like a librarian. She always dresses modestly, but her body seems to rebel against it—ample breasts pushing out the front of her sweaters, lush hips and spectacular ass stretching the wool of her long skirts.

Now and again I'm very tempted to go over and introduce myself, but I'm waiting on her to work up the nerve instead. I don't want to impose on her; she might get scared away. But when I see the longing way she looks at me when she thinks I can't see her…I start thinking about what it would be like to have her.

I haven't had a woman in my life since Jenny's mama died, and she wasn't into the kind of play that I am. I was loyal, so I let that part of myself go unsatisfied. But ever since I've felt ready to move on after Mary, I've been looking for that special someone who won't be satisfied without a good man's firm hand to guide her.

In the bedroom, anyway. Outside of it, I need someone who loves kids and can deal with the rest of my lifestyle. You don't make a billion dollars on legal pot without getting your seed money somewhere a little shady. And once Jenny's off to bed, I still like to smoke every now and then.

It's tough to find someone who's really compatible with everything I am and want. But after the sad mess with Mary, I'm absolutely done with settling. You do that and it doesn't work out, and then you feel like an idiot for making sacrifices for something doomed from the start.

She wasn't a bad person; I loved her, I really did. But she was carrying something besides our baby, something she didn't talk about. Post-partum depression just finally brought it out in her.

I don't like thinking about how she died, or how she tried to take Jenny with her. I'm just glad Jenny was so tiny then that she doesn't remember any of it. I don't hate Mary–but I hate the thing inside of her that made her so horribly crafty and selfish in the end, like a woman possessed.

Now, I stay alone by staying picky. But as I look up to see young Miss Emmeline looking down at me wistfully from her upstairs window, I start to wonder if I couldn't try seeing how we work together. If nothing else, it could make for a very interesting fling.

At this point in my life, I'm hoping for more though. After three and a half years, Jenny is independent and well-behaved enough for us to add to our little family. "Okay, kiddo. Are your eyes closed?"

"Uh-huh!" Jenny has her eyes closed and covered, biting her lip with amusement.

I go to the shed, where I tucked her present shortly before summoning her away from her cartoons, and bring out the covered dog crate within. I set it down next to her, uncover it, and after making sure the gate is locked, I open its door.

The chubby, wagging bundle of golden fur and floppy ears is a pound rescue, with enough Golden Retriever in him that he goes straight for the little girl and flops against her legs, whine-yapping. I fight a grin...and then glance up at Emmeline's window. She's still standing there, smiling wistfully...but definitely smiling.

Two with one stone, I think as I see her looking happy for once. *Or rather, two with one puppy.* "Okay, you can open your eyes."

Jenny uncovers her eyes and looks down...and her jaw drops. "Puppy!" she manages to squeak as the furball bows playfully, his whole butt wagging now. She crouches down and he bounces into her arms, wiggling and licking her face.

"Oh wow it's a doggie! Where'd you get a doggie from? He's so cute!" She bursts out laughing as he starts licking her ears in a frantic, slobbery tickle attack.

"I was waiting until you were old enough. But you have to help me look after him, okay? And he's gonna need a name." I manage to tame my big, stupid grin down into something like a kindly smile.

"I'm gonna think of the best name ever!" She declares, and I lose it, snickering.

"Okay, come on, you guys go play and get to know each other. It'll get cold soon." I keep a careful eye on them as they dash across the lawn together.

I have to admit that watching the two of them wrestle and chase each other does me a hell of a lot of good on this dreary day. It puts all thoughts of Mary, what she did to herself, and what she almost did to my baby, right out of my head.

Jenny and the pup are finally starting to wind down when I notice a gold Mercedes screech to a stop outside of Emmeline's house. An overdressed woman in a scarlet suit—who looks a little like Emmeline if she'd had seven years of cocaine abuse to age her—gets out and stalks up to bang on the gate.

My eyes narrow suspiciously. *Shit, what is this now?*

After a minute or two of nonstop, insistent banging, Emmeline emerges from the front door, a dark coat wrapped around her and a wary look on her face. I keep half an eye on the little ones while I eavesdrop, ears pricked for trouble in my neighborhood.

"What are you doing here?" Emmeline sighs, barely audible.

"You left in the middle of our conversation. I have news from the lawyer. I wanted to make certain that you received it before the day is over." The woman's voice sounds a little like Emmeline's as well, but with an alarming, icy snootiness to it.

"The lawyer?" Emmeline hesitates.

I can tell that whoever this relative of hers is, she's an unwanted visitor—probably because she's a complete bitch. But family legal matters are important. I wince in sympathy as she reluctantly opens the gate and leads the woman inside.

A cold, wary feeling tightens my stomach. I look over at the two new playmates, who are dozing off on the lawn despite the cold. "All right, you two," I announce in a cheery voice as I scoop a kid up with one arm and a puppy with the other. "Let's get you inside to finish watching cartoons. I'll get the doggie crate in a minute."

"Can we have hot chocolate later?" Jenny yawns as I cart her inside.

"You and me can have hot chocolate, sweetie, but this little guy can't. Chocolate's bad for dogs."

I drop them off in front of the TV, make sure I've puppy-proofed everything enough that they'll be fine for a few minutes, and then slip back outside, ears pricked for trouble next door.

I've barely shut the dog crate and scooped it up to take it inside when I hear raised voices over there. One is hard and harsh; the other shakes and is full of sadness and outrage. The very thought of cute little Emmeline sounding so unhappy pisses me off, and I set the crate down and head for the side yard that separates our properties.

Walking alongside the stone fence on my way to the front yard, I can hear the argument growing so loud and impassioned that I'm starting to be able to make out words.

"Only let you in because you said the lawyer—" comes Emmeline's voice. I speed up a little. My gut is telling me that she's not safe.

I trust my instincts. Back in my old business, they kept me alive more than once.

"Bullshit! You were going to the convent and were giving up your share! That money should be mine!" The other woman's screech is so clear that I can only imagine how ear-splitting it must be face-to-face.

"That money was left to me by Mom and Dad, same as yours was to you, you greedy bitch! Get out of my face and get out of my home! I never planned to give it to you anyway, you're rich enough and you have our house!"

I break into a jog, the muscles in my shoulders tightening. As proud as I am that Emmeline's standing up for herself, I know what the long silence that follows her angry statement means. I can feel the tension building next door, like the calm before a storm.

Whoever this other woman is, she's selfish and greedy, and

from the unbalanced screech in her voice, there's no limit to her rage. I don't want her alone with Emmeline right now, even though I barely know the girl.

I'm at a dead run by the time the screaming starts up again. I take the front steps two at a time, and start banging on the door.

3

EMMELINE

"Get out of my home. Get out!" I don't know where this courage is coming from, but I'm chasing Shayla out, step by determined step, while she gives ground slowly toward the door. Her face is dark red with anger, almost the color of her suit, but I can see the fear in her eyes.

I'm going to throw up once she's gone. My stomach churns with each step I take and I'm shaking, my hands cold. But I refuse to show any of these signs of weakness to her. She isn't used to me fighting back, and her surprise right now is the only weapon that I have.

"I'm the oldest!" she's yelling nonsensically. "I'm the heir, and I don't care what their will says. I'll contest it in court!"

"What the hell do you think this is?" I demand as I continue to herd her back into the front hallway. "Medieval Britain? The 'firstborn' thing only mattered then if you had a penis, anyway! And you can contest whatever you want, but all it will do is waste your time and the money you love so much on lawyer fees!"

That makes her hesitate, which disgusts and angers me even more. "I'm not going to let you bully me into giving up what

Mom and Dad left to me like you bullied me into leaving our house! It's my money, this is my home, and you're not my superior. For God's sake, Shayla, you need to go back to therapy and stop–!"

She goes from purple to white and back again. "Don't you fucking talk to me about therapy, Miss Depressed! I'm fine! It's not my fault you could never handle someone with a stronger personality than yours!"

"Being a pushy bitch doesn't make you strong, Shayla. If you were strong you'd be enjoying what you have instead of coming after what's mine." My eyes are locked with hers, while inside I marvel at my own unexpected courage.

"It's all mine!" She shrieks suddenly, and lunges for me, making me freeze with shock. But she doesn't even touch me before a heavy, insistent knock at the door startles us both.

I turn, but Shayla, her anger redirected as quickly as a mad dog's, darts past me and yanks the door open. "Who are you? Fuck off!"

Carl is standing there, arms folded, a thunderous scowl on his face as he stares at Shayla.

I freeze, stunned, unable to understand why in the hell he's on my doorstep when he's taken no interest in me for months. That I know of, anyway. But suddenly, here he is like a white knight, giving her such a forbidding look that all the bluster goes out of her at once.

"W-what are you doing here?" she challenges shakily. She folds her skinny arms and lifts her chin, as if it's her house and he just interrupted something sane and normal. But he's not buying it, and she can tell—and that scares her, too.

Good.

"I heard screaming over here," he rumbles, his voice so unlike the kind tone he uses with his daughter that it sends a small chill down my spine. "I wanted to make sure that Miss Emmeline was not in danger from some…intruder."

Shayla switches gears, going all fluttery and flustered, half of it a smokescreen, but some of it appearing genuine. "Oh no, no, no, I'm actually Emmeline's older sister. We were just having a…private…family discussion–"

"Private? If you wanted to have a private discussion, why could I hear every word from inside my kitchen?"

That seems to get through to Shayla finally. That's always been her way, to thrive on the uncomfortable silence of a family that is forced to tolerate her. Shocked comments from the neighbors, from a visiting friend, from her own boyfriend…all of them break that silence, and throw a spotlight on her behavior.

I'm still mortified that he felt the need to step in, and that this is how we're meeting for the first time: me fighting tears and nausea, and with my heartless nut of a sister standing between us. But as Shayla rubs her face convulsively in response, Carl looks past her and stares right at me…and his whole face changes.

He gives me a sympathetic look, with the tiniest apologetic smile. As if he's been there, dealing with irrational people who teeter at all times on the edge of becoming dangerous. And I realize—with a surge of gratitude and relief—that he didn't come here to yell at me. He came here to save me from the person who was yelling at me.

I bite my lip and nod back, forcing a tiny smile even as my eyes start to sting dangerously. I've become unaccustomed to kindness now that Mom and Dad are gone. It feels good and hurts at the same time. The feeling mixes with my anguish at dealing with Shayla like an antidote, destroying it and restoring some of my strength.

Shayla puts her hand over her mouth and mumbles, all fake modesty, "Oh, I-I-I didn't realize. I…."

"Shayla," I sigh suddenly, my voice stony and exasperated. "Just go away already. You've already embarrassed us both, and you're not four. You're not going to get your way by throwing a tantrum."

She shoots me a look of pure hatred and frustration, and then suddenly scuttles out, shoving the screen door open and shouldering rudely past Carl. He steps aside to let her go, watching her flee down the walk with a bemused look on his face.

We watch silently until she roars off in her gold Mercedes, as if we're both wary of what she'll do until we can see she's gone for good. Then Carl turns back to me, and his sympathetic look returns. "You okay?" he asks very gently.

I draw in a shivery breath and let my heartbeat slow a little before trying to speak. "Yeah," I murmur, giving him the bravest smile I can manage. "I am now. Thank you." I'm so embarrassed that this is how we are finally meeting that I feel like I have to explain myself. "She's...not very rational."

"I noticed." He offers an enormous hand. "We only met briefly at that block party last month, but uh...I've noticed you around. Thought about saying hello, but you seem like a pretty private person."

I hesitate, then clasp his hand with my own as best I can. His enormous hand closes over mine and surrounds it in brief, leathery warmth. It's all I can do not to whimper at his comforting touch.

"Y-yeah, sorry I left early that day. I was going to introduce myself but the crowd got kind of overwhelming after a while." I blame Shayla. I was afraid of running into her in that crowd, after a week of obsessive phone calls out of nowhere. If that hadn't happened, maybe I could have spent a little more time at the block party, and become friends with the neighbors I still don't really know.

Like Carl.

The warmth of his hand sinks into mine, and for a long moment, I linger, wishing I could keep holding hands with him without seeming like a weirdo. Finally, I let him go. "I wish the circumstances were better, but I'm glad we've finally introduced ourselves properly."

His smile goes a touch cheerier. Then he points over his shoulder at his house. "Hey, uh, I can't leave my kid. You want to come over for some cocoa?"

I blink at him, the homey offer sounding strange coming out of a gigantic tough guy like him. He seems to know it and chuckles sheepishly, shoving his hands in his pockets. "Can't break out the booze until after my kid's in bed. It's a rule."

"Oh that's all right. I could really use some chocolate right now, actually." I step out onto the porch, fishing in my pocket for my keys. Shayla is gone, but until the smell of her perfume dissipates from the rooms of my house, I don't want to be there.

And as for Carl…he could ask me to go to the garbage dump with him, and I would probably say yes.

"So does she hassle you like that a lot?" he asks quietly as I finish locking up and turn to follow him back to his house.

"Since I was three. She has a kind of mental disorder—and she's a complete bitch on top of that."

He opens the gate for me. "Maybe you should get a restraining order. I don't want to get in your business uninvited, but if she's been this way for almost twenty years, she's not gonna change."

His garden is immaculate, populated with nontoxic trees and flowers to go with its clover and chamomile lawn. Even his yard is kid-safe. I wonder if he redid the landscaping himself.

I drink in the sight and scents, letting them soothe me. "I know," I reply once I've centered myself a little. "It's part of why I moved out of our family home. But she doesn't seem to be satisfied with just driving me away."

"If she's as narcissistic as she seems, they're all like that." His tone is tired and knowing as he leads me up onto the porch. His house is twice the size of mine, the porch double-deep beneath a matching wraparound balcony. "Narcissists drive people away with their behavior, but then they get desperate for attention and go chasing after them."

"Sounds like you're speaking from experience," I comment as he unlocks his door. He nods mutely, an ironic smile ghosting across his face as he looks back over his shoulder.

Maybe he's right and I should get a protection order against Shayla. I'm tired of this.

A blast of warm air hits me in the face as I step in behind him. It smells of toasted bread, mint, and faintly of damp doggie. No sooner is the door shut than two small figures race out of the living room, one dressed in pink, the other in gold fur.

The latter, all wagging tail and flailing paws, pounces on my shoe, and I feel the last of my tension dissolve as I watch the little guy untie it with his little black-jowled mouth. "Well, hi there!"

"Daddy, you promised cocoa," the tiny blonde imp clinging to Carl's leg pouts slightly and then turns to look at me. "Hi, did you come to see my new puppy?"

"Hi! I'm Emmeline. Um, I'm your neighbor. Your dad invited me over for cocoa." I reach down and scratch the puppy's ears, and he starts trying to engulf my fingertips in his mouth.

"That's a pretty name. I'm Jenny. My daddy's named Carl, but you can call him Daddy."

Carl suddenly bursts into a coughing fit, harrumphing and pressing a fist against his mouth.

"Um. Okay, thanks for that?" I smile awkwardly, wondering what Carl finds so funny, and why he's hiding his laughter.

4
CARL

Something about this whole Shayla situation stinks, but I'm too busy being glad that Emmeline and I are finally talking, that for a while, the ugly truth doesn't sink in. But minutes later, when I'm stirring melted chocolate into milk and listening to Jenny brag about her new dog to our neighbor, I feel my hackles go up. Long experience tells me that Emmeline's hiding just how bad the situation with her sister is.

I don't know if Shayla is a cokehead or just naturally unstable. My guess either way is that she's a typical abuser: deep down she knows that what she is doing is wrong, and tries to keep it under wraps in public to avoid criticism, which she clearly cannot stand.

I've dealt with tons of coke-fueled narcissists and paranoids before. During the early noughties it seemed like every single grower from Mexico to Jamaica to Humboldt was snorting half their profits to "keep sharp." I would show up to make my pickup, and some twitchy, argumentative addict would start fucking with me over price, amounts, packaging, and every other damn thing.

Cocaine confidence makes crazy idiots out of people, which

is part of why I never touch or sell anything besides pot. Cokeheads always think they're the masters of the universe while they're flying, only to turn into desperate assholes as soon as they touch down. Either way, you're dealing with an irrational person who nine times out of ten will be a dick just to watch how it affects you.

It's even worse when they're related to you.

I only know that one second-hand, though. I don't have much in the way of family. I've got some cousins out of state that I grew up with, and I check in on Mary's mom to let her see her granddaughter every week or so.

She's a nice lady—and hurt as hell over what Mary did. We had that in common, though I've finally made my peace with it.

I've committed myself to helping her feel a little less alone. Propping "Gramma Carol" up and looking after my little girl helped me get through. It's a lot easier to be strong through a heartbreak when you're being strong for someone else.

I sigh and keep stirring, knowing that if I let the cocoa boil it will separate and get nasty. Easier to throw a packet of some chalky stuff into warm milk, but that's not how I roll. Not with my little girl, and not with my hot, adorable, and very distressed guest.

Emmeline might be bearing up well, but I can tell she's suffering under it all. Her voice is almost overly gentle right now as she talks to my daughter in the other room. Now and again it grows a little breathless.

I wonder how many times she turns her head to check the windows while I'm in here making cocoa. She did it constantly when I was in the room with them.

I wonder if she's checking for Shayla, and if so, if Shayla is actually the sort to lurk at strangers' windows. If I do find her out there, I'll call my buddy Jake at the precinct to come take care of it. Better that than give in to the temptation to pitch her over the fence like a sack of trash.

When I walk in with two mugs and one insulated sippy cup of hot cocoa, the dog gets underfoot, excited at the new smell. Jenny giggles, and Emmeline gets up to corral the little guy before I can trip over him. "Thanks," I grump good-naturedly as I set down the tray on our cherry coffee table.

Jenny toddles over with her hands out and nearly gets tripped by the dog herself. Emmeline grabs the little beast again and wrestles with him while Jenny rights herself and takes her prize, immediately taking a swallow. This is why I always cool hers with an extra dollop of milk.

"You come up with a name for this furball yet, sweetie?" I ask my daughter as she climbs back onto the recliner across from the couch.

"Flubber!" she declares, and I burst into incredulous laughter. Emmeline settles onto the far end of the couch, chuckling quietly.

"Flubber? Why are you gonna call your dog that?" It's cute and hilarious, and better than Doggie-face, which was her first idea for a name.

"Because he bounces!" she declares, and I can't help but laugh more.

"Flubber it is. Just don't complain about it when you're ten and he's eighty pounds."

"I won't! C'mon, Flubber!" She pats the seat next to her and the dog scrambles up to settle in beside her, snuffling at the cup. He loses interest after a few moments, the insulation and narrow opening masking most of the chocolate scent.

"They're so cute." Emmeline is smiling, really smiling, and the sight of it warms me more than my drink. "How long have you lived here?"

"Two and a half years. It was a mess when I got here. Had to fix it up so it was good enough for my little girl." I scratch the corner of my jaw thoughtfully as I look at her. "How about you? Where were you before this?"

"Garden District. I grew up there. Mom and Dad both have family here going back a couple of hundred years." She smiles faintly, her velvety dark eyes hiding demurely behind her lashes. A true Creole beauty, with deep roots that I find myself envying.

"A real New Orleans native, huh?" It's hard not to smile now that we're finally in the same room together, even though part of my mind keeps chewing over the scene with Shayla the whole time.

I need to talk with her about this. As much as I'd like to be her personal hero, even if nothing ever happens between us, this is my street. I won't let anybody get hurt in my territory, even if she's just a friendly neighbor.

"That's me. I don't think I'll ever want to leave. I mean, maybe part of the year. The summers do get really hot up here."

"When it gets too bad, I usually take Jenny and go off in my plane for a month or two to my farmlands in Oregon. We come back after the last harvest and processing are done, which is usually late fall." It's a lot to tell her about myself in one go, but since I now know so many private things about her, it seems fair to open up a bit.

"You're a farmer? I thought you were an ex-soldier or something." She's intrigued, and I take that as a good sign.

"Ex-pilot, actually. I used to run my own delivery company." Close enough to the truth. "I own a hundred acres in Humboldt County, got a buddy managing it for me."

"Humboldt?" Her eyebrows rise. She's heard of it—of course. Everybody who has ever smoked bud at least once has heard of it. "Oh."

"Do you think Flubber's a good name?" Jenny breaks in after running out of cocoa to drain from her sippy. She sets it aside, leaving the puppy to nose at it curiously, and peers at Emmeline earnestly.

"Flubber is a lovely name, sweetheart. Don't let your daddy give you a hard time." She shoots me a mischievous look that's a pleasant surprise. Her mood's recovering. That makes me feel good—too good, maybe.

Maybe if I work hard enough, I can get her mind entirely off of Shayla...and on me instead.

"I can't believe she even remembers that movie," I admit, a little baffled. When did I even watch it with her?

"Well, it must have stuck." Emmeline is sipping her cocoa a lot more slowly than I, her hands laced carefully around the heavy ceramic mug, as if worried she will fumble it. She does still glance at the front windows now and again, whenever the breeze moves the branches of the mulberry tree and casts a shadow on the glass.

I get the impression that she's rarely at rest, and she probably doesn't sleep very well either. *Maybe I can help there too?*

Looking at Emmeline as she holds a friendly little conversation with my daughter about dog names, I want to do a lot more than just take her to my bed. I want to protect her. I want to make sure she can sleep at night, and feel safe during the day. I want to make her smile....

Damn it, hold up. I barely know this woman, and here I am already imagining her in my collar.

I have to watch that. If there's one thing I have a problem with when it comes to women, it's falling too hard for them, too fast. Especially the kind ones.

The warm milk in the cocoa is doing its work, as did all the excited running around with the new puppy. Jenny yawns enormously, and I look over at her. "That's yawn number one, sweetie."

"I'm not sleepy," she mumbles—and then stifles another yawn. The puppy is already draped over her lap, blinking slowly.

"All right, but you know the rules. One more yawn and I'll have to shuffle you off to bed for your nap."

"I know," she mumbles—and yawns again before I can even look away from her.

"Gimme just a minute," I say to Emmeline, who nods and takes another dainty sip of her cocoa. Her eyes dance slightly with amusement as I scoop up kid and pup and turn to bring them upstairs. The dog wiggles a little, but Jenny is already starting to doze.

Once Jenny is tucked in with her shoes off and Flubber in her arms, I go back down to check on my guest. The weight of what I have to ask her tugs at my chest. This isn't going to be easy, but I won't feel right until it's done.

"How's she doing?" she asks softly, her sympathy as honest and easy as if we've been close for years.

"Out like a light. She'll sleep until almost supper time after all the running around she's done today." Chasing Jenny is starting to become a real effort. I'm fit, fast, and tireless, but three-year-olds are giggling blurs.

I sit back down on the couch, settle back into my seat, and scoop up my mug. "Look, I don't want to invade your privacy, but I think that we need to talk about what happened with your sister today."

She looks down and away at once, a blush deepening on her cheeks. "I'm sorry. I didn't ever want you to have to deal with Shayla and her bullshit."

"Why are you apologizing to me?" I ask, baffled. "Look, I brought it up because I'm concerned for you and your safety. You're my neighbor, and I'd want to help you even if I didn't like you or think you're cute as hell."

Her eyes widen, and after a moment I realize I probably said a little bit too much, given how long we've known each other. Still, it's true, and at least it gives her some idea of my motives. Okay, they're not perfect—but they're honest, and they do involve giving a damn about her.

"Look, like I said, I don't mean to embarrass you or get too personal. But I have known people like Shayla before, and they only ever become more bothersome. Are you sure you're even safe with her around?"

She sets her mug down a little hard. Her hands are shaking, and tears spill over her eyes. She wipes at them self-consciously. "Wow, my mascara's really getting a workout today," she mumbles.

I feel terrible for a moment…until I catch the relief in her expression.

"I'm sorry," she says in a shaky voice. "It's just that you're the first person to give this much of a damn about me since my parents died."

"Holy shit, I'm sorry. Don't you have any friends?" Somehow, though, that just makes her look more miserable, and my heart sinks. *Think I just put my foot in my mouth there.*

"I'd like to have friends," she admits after a moment, "but I don't have any practice."

"What, why? Shayla?" It has to be Shayla.

"She would always drive them away," comes the soft reply, disgusting me. "I tried to have friends, but if Shayla caught me hanging out with someone she would bully both of us until they avoided me. She wanted all my attention so she could…" She trails off, her voice rising to a squeak before the tears come again and she closes her eyes.

"Have you all to herself. But then she drove you away?" I'm trying to get a grasp on Shayla's character, like I would suss out an enemy, or a potential betrayer. It was a necessary skill in my old business—always keep one eye out for a knife headed for your back.

"She wanted me to give up my half of our childhood home so she could keep the whole thing. She drove me here, and then that wasn't enough so she followed me." Her chest is heaving distractingly, but the tears in her eyes make the luscious display impossible to enjoy.

"It's like I said. Is she on cocaine? She reminds me of a person on coke." She might get curious as to how I know that, but right now, I just don't care.

"She might be, I don't know. She's so much bolder now that Mom and Dad are gone and she has money." She sniffles, and then looks up at me suddenly. "Why *do* you care?"

Her voice isn't accusing, but rather full of a desperate plea—but it has the same basic effect. The question freezes me in my tracks, not because I'm uncertain of my answer, but because I'm uncertain of how she'll take it.

Go gently, I tell myself, draining the rest of my mug before answering.

"It's exactly like I said. You're my neighbor, I like you, and I'm attracted to you. But more than that, I want my neighbors to be safe no matter how biased toward or against them I am."

"So you...look after the neighborhood?"

I nod. That's a good enough way of putting it. "My little girl needs to grow up in a neighborhood where people look after each other. Only way to get people to do that is to lead by example."

Her eyes search my face, and then she slowly nods. "It's been a while since I met anyone like that," she admits, and I can only give her a sad smile.

She sips at her cocoa, her gaze going from me to the windows and back again, her lush body drawn up tighter than usual. "I used to spy on the family therapists when they would be talking to my family. I was trying to figure out why Shayla is the way she is.

"She would drive doctors away just like everyone else, and they could never agree on how to treat her. But they gave a bunch of diagnoses that explained some of her behavior.

"They kept stressing that none of this excused her being that nasty and selfish. She refused to do anything that would help her cope with her personality disorders. They just became her excuse to be such a selfish, unkind person."

My lips twist and I look down. How many sad sons-of-bitches have I known who dove into drugs and stupid behavior while blaming their wartime PTSD, or their addiction, or any of the rest of it for their personal choices? I feel bad for them and what they carry, but most of the time, being sick has never been a get-out-of-responsibility-free card in my book.

My attitude about that is the only thing that helped me get over Mary's death and the terrible way she treated me and her own mother in the months before it. Maybe she thought she was doing us a favor by severing ties before her death, but love and loyalty don't work that way. I kept fighting for her, and she broke my fucking heart—especially when she tried to take our daughter with her.

If my daughter ever asks me about her mother's suicide, I'll tell her that her mom had a disease and couldn't help herself. But Mary's suicide wasn't an impulse. It was meticulously planned, and from the start, it involved trying to kill Jenny too.

I'm fucking sick of people using their problems as an excuse to destroy other people's lives. It's not their fault they're sick, but letting a wound fester never helps it heal, and when your sickness can harm a lot of people, it's irresponsible not to try to get a handle on it.

"I know exactly what you mean. I had a few people close to

me act a lot like this. The stuff Shayla's doing is familiar to me... and that's why I'm so worried."

The blush is back. It's so damn cute that I pause for a moment to just look at her. But it still makes me a little sad. "Wow, you're really not used to people giving a shit about you outside your parents, huh?"

"No," she mumbles.

"Well, get used to it." I look at her right in those soft brown eyes and see her blush deepen as she struggles to keep eye contact. It's adorable...but right now, I'm deadly serious.

She just stares at me, managing a nod but nothing else.

I take a deep breath, compelled to explain myself. "People like Shayla try to isolate you from any support system so they don't have to face real push-back for their actions. It's calculated. I don't want a person who thinks and acts like that in my neighborhood, causing problems for you and yelling so loud she scares my kid. So unless you tell me to fuck off and let you deal with it all yourself, I want to be your backup. The person you go to if there's a problem."

I see her hesitate, and I understand that hesitation more than she probably thinks. Every time someone offers me a deal that seems too good to be true, I'm skeptical.

She chews her full lip nervously, and I wish to God I could just take her into my arms and tell her that she'll be all right from now on. That I'll take care of her.

Instead, I let the offer stand, and let her consider it undistracted for a while.

"I...would feel safer if I had someone close by I could go to," she finally says, and I struggle to hide my relief. "You're right... she's only gotten worse over time. I really didn't feel safe today while she was in my house."

"Then your instincts are good. There are very few things more dangerous than when a person like that realizes you won't take their shit anymore. Some get scared off, but others fly off the rails."

She pales then, and I realize that I've touched a crucial nerve. "She was reaching for me when you banged on the door," she murmurs breathlessly.

Fuck.

"Okay," I reply gravely. "In that case, I'm gonna have to insist. If she starts causing you any kind of trouble again, showing up uninvited or anything like that, then you come to me. All right?"

She swallows, guilt and hesitation clouding her face. After a moment she takes a deep breath and it clears, and she smiles softly in relief. "Thank you."

5

EMMELINE

My phone beeps again, and I see that I have another message. Shayla has been calling. She's been calling all night. But it doesn't matter anymore, because I'm protected.

Carl is making everything better. Well, not everything. I'm sure I have years of therapy ahead of me from dealing with that harpy, not to mention what happened to Mom and Dad. But that's all right, because if Shayla causes any real problems beyond just whining, I have someone I can call.

The best someone.

If I had a little crush on this guy before, it's at ridiculous levels now. I left his house smiling, and I feel like I'm floating two inches off the floor just thinking about it as I move around my kitchen.

The phone beeps—another message. I make myself green tea with honey.

The phone beeps—I don't even look at it as I sip my tea. It beeps again twice before I finish my first cup. I pour myself a second.

My thoughts are preoccupied with Carl. The warm glow I feel drowns out any anxiety over making Shayla angry. He cares. *He wants to protect me.*

He even called me cute and said he was attracted to me! How did I get so lucky? It's always possible that he's messing with me, but he just doesn't seem the type.

No, there's no room in my heart right now for fearing Shayla or worrying about what she'll do. My stomach's doing little flips, but the apprehension is mixed with wild excitement.

What if Carl asks me out on a date?

The thought of it leaves me sitting there daydreaming while my second cup of tea goes cold. I never dated much as a teen, and not at all once I decided to join a convent after junior college. Now I'm left wondering...what would being with Carl be like?

"Being with,"...crap, I sound like a fourteen-year-old. I'm thinking about dating him. Kissing him. Fucking him—though I have no idea what that is like. But I'd love to find out.

The phone beeps again, and I hesitate. I've been letting my voicemail fill up with Shayla's tantrums and threats, gathering evidence. I hate having to prepare to get a protection order against my own sister, but it's her fault, not mine.

Finally, I give up and scoop up my phone. I stare at the message screen—she's filled the mailbox completely. I save the messages to my cloud without listening to them, delete them off my phone, and then—after months of not having enough nerve—I block Shayla's number.

Eventually, she'll buy other phones to call me from, and she'll start hassling me all over again. But it will take her time, and she's lazy. It means I can at least spend tonight in peace.

Thank God. I could really use the break.

This is the first time since my parents died that I have felt even a little bit safe. And it's all because of Carl. It's nice to know that I once again have someone who will look out for me and help me deal with the world—to know that I'm not all alone.

Things might not turn out as well as I'm hoping. But if he doesn't ask me out, then I'm darn well going to have to work up the nerve to do it myself. *Now how do I do that?*

I'll have to start small, or I'll lose my nerve entirely. And I will have to work around his schedule, because I know he'd never abandon Jenny. *So...coffee?*

I look around my house, with half the rooms bare still except for stacked-up boxes. I need to get to work unpacking and fixing everything up if I'm going to have guests. I'm suddenly embarrassed by all those weeks of doing only a box or so a day, no matter how hard of a time I was having.

Would Carl understand? Probably. But that doesn't stop me from wanting to put a better face forward. Especially now that his offer of friendship and protection has made me feel better than I have in months.

I'm able to unpack the living room and get the dining room table and chairs put together that night before I run out of steam. It's a big step. I could be ready to have Carl over in a day or two. If I can just get my downstairs together, it won't matter if the spare bedroom and my office are still in boxes.

At least my bedroom is done already, if he ends up upstairs. But that thought just makes me blush like crazy all over again.

My arms ache as I bring the last load of broken-down boxes to my recycling bin outside. I need a shower and some more sleep. But I'm smiling, both proud of myself and grateful for this small turn in my lonely life. I'm still smiling half an hour later, when I climb into bed with my still-damp hair freshly braided.

The knocking wakes me up a few hours later.

I tense and roll over, listening to the continuous, insistent banging as the fog clears from my head. It could be Shayla—or maybe the police, calling to tell me she rolled her car while throwing a tantrum in traffic. After a few moments' hesitation, I get up and look down at my front curb.

Shayla's gold Mercedes is sitting there—still running, lights on, driver's side door hanging open. Her parking is even shittier than usual, with one wheel up on the curve, turned at an angle to the street. As the sight registers, I hear her voice yell up "Emmeline!"

I freeze in indecision. *Call the police? Call Carl? Go down and tell her to fuck off?*

I take a deep breath, feeling my stomach start to curdle again. *It's late. I don't want to irritate Carl by calling, but he insisted.*

It takes me three tries to bring myself to phone him.

He picks up on the first ring. "Hi, I'm sorry to bother you," I start, but he cuts me off.

"It's fine, I already heard her and saw her car. I'm gonna call a buddy of mine on the force. It may be a bit before he gets there though." His voice is calm, focused—all business.

My blood runs hot and then cold again with my mix of emotions, and I take a shivery breath. "Thank you."

"It's fine, sweetheart, the cops are on their way. Just hold tight. That's a steel-core door, and if I hear any glass break I'll be over in a flash."

"Okay, I uh...I'll stay up here until they show." I chew my lip. I hate the idea of dealing with Shayla's embarrassing behavior in front of the police. But if she does something horrible, and it happens to be illegal, at least I won't have to deal with her for a while.

But I'll have to deal with the aftermath of whatever she does. Please let the police get this under control before I come out.

"Okay. Call me back if you get scared." He hangs up.

Downstairs, the banging continues. Shayla is cursing and calling my name. She sounds drunk. I wonder how she got over here without destroying her car.

I move to the window again to watch her. I don't know how long she has been out there, but it's probably been a while. I'm a light sleeper, but only when something disturbs my immediate space.

Finally, I catch sight of red and blue flashing lights, and stare in amazement. Absently I grab my robe off the back of my chair and wrap it around myself, wondering how in the world Carl got the police to get here so fast. *Thank God for small favors.*

I step into my slippers and make my way down the stairs as the knocking suddenly stops. I can hear the hysterical tone in Shayla's voice as she confronts the police. I don't know what she's saying, but I hope it's something so abusive that she ends up in handcuffs.

I make my way down the stairs and walk up to the front door, hesitating. I can hear Shayla sobbing and whining about something now, in a much lower voice. I open the door with a sense of relief washing through me.

Shayla is standing at the base of my stairs, mascara running down her face, hair askew, hugging herself. Two uniformed cops flank her, looking both tired and a little confused. One of them, a dark-eyed, fox-faced man, turns a stony expression to me.

"There's the bitch, that's her!" Shayla cries suddenly, stabbing an accusing finger in my direction. "My own sister locked me out of our house in the cold!"

I stare at her, so stunned that my heart painfully skips a beat. The rush of adrenaline sends cold needles through me as I watch my sister turn into an expert impersonator again.

"Shayla, why did you change the locks? I live here! I have no place to go!"

I shake back the brief, agonizing flashback, and the irony

pisses me off to no end. "She doesn't live here," I say in a mix of confusion and outrage. Only the confusion is played up. Really, after everything she has done, I should have seen this tactic coming.

Foxface's brows knit together and he looks over at his partner, a mellow-looking Creole man with a carefully trimmed fade beneath his uniform cap. "Have we got a confirmation of their home addresses?"

"I can provide mine, if you need it," I say in the steadiest voice I can manage. My eyes are too blurry from panic and exhaustion to read their name badges, but I manage not to cry or yell at anyone.

My cooperativeness seems to get their attention. Foxface sighs. "Miss Lacroix, as reluctant as we are to get involved in a family manner, your sister here claims that this is her place of residence, and you've locked her out in the cold."

"Um, I'm really sorry that this has happened—," I say immediately, but Shayla cuts me off.

"I can't believe she changed the locks while I was gone! How could you lock me out, Emmeline? I have no place to go!" Her voice rises to a wail in a dramatic mockery of my grief on that night that I slept on the porch—and suddenly there's nothing in my head but rage.

"Officers, please, my sister's ID, mail, and keys will all prove that she lives in our family home in the Garden District." I give them the address. "I moved here after she locked *me* out. Now she is harassing me because I blocked her phone number earlier tonight."

"She's lying!" comes the screech, and I shudder, my heart pounding hard. How in the world does Shayla manage to yell this loud without hurting her throat? "I can't believe this, I know she hates me but this isn't legal! You have to arrest her and let me in!"

I'm shaking now, but I stand my ground. "Half of my things are still in boxes. I just moved here, alone. There's one bed set up, and you know we're not sharing one. I will take you inside and show you, but please, do not let my abuser into my house."

Foxface's eyes light up with sudden understanding, and he and his partner exchange a glance. There's something fiercely knowing in the Foxface's stare—but the other man shakes his head slightly, unimpressed.

The cop in front of me, Foxface, holds up his hands. "Okay, look. How about, I go in, with your permission, have a look around, and you can explain the whole thing. Do you have any—?"

"Hey! Damn it, you stupid cop, why are you talking to her instead of me? She's the one who did something wrong, I told you—"

"Ma'am," his partner growls, "I am talking to you, and Officer Eames is talking to your sister."

"But...but...you should listen to me, not her! I'm the one who called you!" Shayla seems so baffled that I don't know if she's being manipulative, or if she's simply delusional.

"That doesn't mean we know who between the two of you is lying yet," Officer Eames snaps over his shoulder. Shayla sucks in air and I tense, half expecting an explosion. He turns his attention back to me, his expression going neutrally professional again.

Shayla uses the one tiny scrap of wisdom she possesses in not talking back to the cop, and I swallow my disappointment.

"I'm sorry," he says to me, "but it actually would help if I could see the state of your home to corroborate your story. And it would help even more if you had a witness to verify who lives where."

"I'm happy to help with that." A tall, broad-shouldered

shape in a familiar motorcycle jacket walks up to my front gate, speaking in a clear, calm voice. "Carl Black. I live next door."

Shayla lets off whining at Officer Eames's partner and levels a glare of pure hatred at Carl. He offers a cold smile in return—but when he turns to me, his eyes twinkle.

My hero, I think, heart lifting with relief.

6

CARL

From the desperate look on Emmeline's face and the way she sags in relief when she sees me, I know my timing's good. As for my drinking buddy Jamie, who has been our beat cop along with his partner Tom for eighteen months, we exchange a brief glance before he goes back to doing his job. I have to pretend I don't know him well, or Shayla's likely to kick up a stink about corruption.

"Well, sir, we got a phone call from Ms. Lacroix about being locked out of her house by her sister." He gestures at the bitch, who is glaring at me like she wants to murder me right there. I wink at her, and she goes white.

"Locked out of her house? This woman doesn't live here. In fact, I had to tell her to leave this afternoon because she was threatening Emmeline. I could hear her screaming from my kitchen. So could my kid."

I can't imagine the last time I said anything to an on-duty police officer that gave me this much satisfaction. "I've been here two and a half years. She doesn't even live in this neighborhood."

Looking at Shayla's bleary outrage and incredibly shitty

parking job, I put two and two together. "Maybe she's just an aggressive drunk, but twice in one day is too much for me."

"Oh, so drunk and disorderly? And possible drunk driving? Tom, get the breathalyzer." Jamie gives Shayla a knowing look that takes a lot of the wind from her sails. Then he turns back to Emmeline. "We're going to have to document this, but right now, with her behavior, it can only work in your favor if you end up pressing harassment charges."

"I'm getting a protection order," Emmeline speaks up, her voice choked but clear. "She can't just—"

Shayla lets out an incoherent scream and lunges at Emmeline. I leap the gate and bolt across the lawn, but both cops are on it, grabbing her and pulling her back. She starts fighting them, flailing and screaming, while I bound toward Emmeline and pull her out of range.

I gather her against my chest and turn us so my body is between her and her crazed sister. She shivers against my chest, her face pale. "It's okay, sweetheart, just let them do their jobs."

"You can't do this! You can't! This *is* my house! They're *both* my house! I'm the oldest! Everything that bitch has is mine!" I look over and see that Shayla is fighting them with everything she has as they drag her toward the squad car.

"We'll take care of this," Jamie promises. "I'm gonna need statements from all of you, though. Can you take care of things here, and come in to give statements first thing tomorrow?"

Emmeline nods against my chest and I nod at Jamie. "Is nine all right?"

"That's fine. Call me if anything changes." I have no idea how he can keep such a calm tone while stuffing a screeching drunk into the back of his cruiser, but now that the cuffs are on he's doing exactly that to Shayla.

"Fuck you! I'll kill that little bitch! None of you know your place!" She hits her head on the door frame on her way into the car, and threatens Jamie with a few badly-aimed kicks.

"Thank you!" Emmeline manages very shakily, and I start stroking her hair.

Once they're gone, I take Emmeline back to my place to calm down. Jenny greets us at the door with a sleepy puppy leaning against her leg. "What happened?" she frets, bouncing.

Crap. I'd hoped that she would sleep through this mess like she does almost anything else, but looks like I miscalculated. "I'm sorry, baby," I say as I bring Emmeline through the door. "I had to help Emmeline with a problem."

"Okay." She frowns in worry as she sees Emmeline's tear-streaked face. I close the door behind us, and she chirps, "Who was that loud lady?"

"My sister," Emmeline replies softly as I lead her over to the couch and help her settle onto it.

"Oh." Jenny thinks about it a moment, then smiles. "You're nice. I'm sorry your sister's bad."

Emmeline lets go of me reluctantly as she sits down. "Me too, sweetie. I'm sorry she woke you up."

"I have to get her settled again," I apologize to Emmeline, who smiles tearfully and nods.

"Go ahead. I'll manage now that she's gone."

I peer at her, wary of a martyr streak. "You sure you're okay?"

She nods. "I'll be fine." She turns to Jenny, who is waving as I scoop her into my arms.

"Goodnight, sweetie. The bad woman's gone, so you try and rest now, okay?"

"Okay!" Jenny says perkily. I walk out with her as she waves over my shoulder, the puppy bumbling along behind us.

I'm a lucky guy. My little girl doesn't freak out at the prospect of a nut bothering the neighborhood. She trusts me when I say she's safe, and she's sleeping peacefully within five minutes.

When I come back down, Emmeline has calmed down a lot. She sits on my couch with her hands in her lap, and I realize for the first time that she's in my home in nothing but her nightgown, slippers, and robe. Blue and cream. Cute, and—fortunately for her—warm. But the glimpses of her shape underneath make it sexy.

"Are you okay?" I ask her as gently as I can. She swallows and nods, and I settle onto the couch nearby. "Can I do anything for you?"

"Um," she looks at the ceiling, eyes tearing up again. "You've already done so much."

"I do it because I want to," I reassure, and she smiles briefly, with a touch of embarrassment. "No, seriously, don't think you owe me something. Even if you weren't hot, and kind, *and* adorable, I would do this. Thought I covered that already."

"I'm just not used to it, not since my dad died. I'm...very sorry if I make it awkward." Our eyes meet briefly, and I see the shame and pain in hers and hold up a hand.

"No, seriously. Just assume you can ask me for anything. If it bothers me, or if I can't do it, I will let you know. Okay? I'm being completely straight with you right now."

She bites her lip softly, and I feel my mouth go dry. But I wait quietly, and finally she says, "Actually, there is one thing...."

She asks me to do something I'd actually wanted to do anyway—check her house for intruders, since she had not had time to properly lock up. Once I get some tea in her and she's feeling well enough, we go back to her front door.

"I'll go in first," I insist. "Trail back at least a few paces."

She nods obediently and I give her a smile. *Good girl.* I have to force myself away from wondering if she takes direction just as well in bed.

I clear each room, checking everywhere a human could hide, before letting Emmeline into it. The house is only ten rooms, including the finished attic and both bathrooms. It doesn't take long to find...absolutely nothing.

And that's a good thing.

"Okay, sweetheart," I tell her as I return to her. "All clear."

"Thank you," she murmurs again. "I don't know what I would have done without you here." She sniffles, and I see tears start to gleam on her cheeks again.

"Hey," I say softly, moving forward to lay my hands on her shoulders as we stand in the upper hallway. "Don't you think about that, because I was here. I'll always be here, sweetheart."

She smiles through her tears, and I hug her against me again. It feels so fucking good to hold her. The smell of her hair, that jasmine perfume, her warmth, the way she shivers against me. How long has it been since I've had a woman in my arms that I actually care for? *Years. Since Mary.*

She makes a sudden, soft sound of pleasure, and I don't fully know why until I realize I'm totally absorbed in the warm, wet softness of her full lips against mine. Her body arches up against me, breasts pushing into my chest through my shirt, and I feel my cock stir to life as my grip on her tightens.

She's clinging to me, trembling, her body pressed urgently against mine. That jasmine perfume mixes with the faint musk of her body, enticing me further. I know without a doubt that she wants this. But...why is she trembling so hard?

I break the kiss very reluctantly and look down at her, murmuring, "You all right, sweetheart?"

"Just a little dizzy," she admits, looking a little embarrassed. "I'm sorry. I've actually never done this before."

My mind and body immediately go into total war against each other as I realize she's *untouched* as well as untrained. I might be her first real crush ever—maybe even her first kiss.

She's scared and overwhelmed, exhausted...and entirely new

at this. I'm not going to take advantage—no matter how badly I want her.

Instead, I stroke her loose hair back from her face as I smile down at her. "We'll take things slow, then. I don't want to push you into anything you're not comfortable with."

My cock aches for her, but I force myself to loosen my grip. I will keep my word. I will let her set the pace, gently pushing at her limits, not bulldozing them.

I see the relief hiding in her smile, and the trust, and I know that I have made the right choice.

7
EMMELINE

I've never experienced a kiss like this in my life. I've been kissed impulsively by men before, but not the kind of deep, passionate embrace that I've been dreaming about for months. My whole body tingles; every inch of my attention collapses inward toward the feel of his mouth on mine. I don't even remember when I start clinging to him, but I know for certain that I would be a puddle on the floor if it weren't for his arms around me.

When I get overwhelmed, it embarrasses me. The flood of sensation, this unexpected closeness, the passion in his kiss, all of it feels incredible—but there's too much pleasure, naked and raw, so much that it edges on pain. Nerve endings that have never been used tingle uncomfortably as my heart pounds and I start to lose control of myself.

He shocks me with his understanding, and offers to take it slow. I'm breathless and shaky as I nod my agreement. When he leaves my house, I lie awake for hours, remembering the taste of his mouth.

I let myself sleep in a little, knowing that I'm safe and that no matter what happens, Shayla can't get at me right now. Even if she pays her bail, she's being watched by the police.

My alarm wakes me again at seven thirty. I feel bleary and fog-headed from the lack of sleep, but we're due at the police precinct at nine, and I have to get ready.

In the shower, the hot water stinging my skin reminds me so much of how I felt with Carl that it makes me dizzy. That kiss is going to haunt me for weeks. It's a welcome memory.

I'm smiling as I make my way downstairs. Carl hasn't messaged me yet, but it's eight thirty and I'm sure he will soon. I'm so happy and relieved to have his help—and to have felt his kiss—that I don't even look through the peephole when the doorbell rings. I just pull the door open.

A total stranger is standing on the other side.

I freeze, blinking out at the man in white who stands with a mild smile on his face just inches from my screen door. He has a door-to-door evangelist's blandly cheerful smile on his pale, pretty face, and his pale blue eyes gleam flatly, his brown curls tousled just so. "Hi there," he says around that odd smile. "I'm Roland from the diocese."

My fear fades a fraction—but not that much. I'm not expecting anyone, and I'm absolutely certain that the diocese would have called before they sent someone. "Can I help you?" I ask tentatively, still too shocked to sort out my feelings on the sudden intrusion.

"Yes, well, the Mother Superior you were working with spoke with us about your current crisis of faith. I wanted to know if you would like to discuss it before making any final decisions about your life as a Catholic and as a candidate for the convent."

His language is very generalized. Alarm bells start to ring in my head. I don't want to be rude, but...this isn't normal.

"I'm very sorry," I say in the politest tone I can muster, "But I have an important appointment and will be leaving in a few minutes. Would you like to leave your card, and I'll arrange something with you after I get back?"

The smile freezes on his face, and I feel worry wash through me. I can't pinpoint exactly why, I just know that something in his expression stands as a warning. Maybe it's the fact that his eyes never change expression.

"I'm afraid that this is the only time I have in your area," he replies smoothly, his eyes raking me over. It makes me even more nervous. I feel a strange tension rising inside of me as my manners and my caution clash.

"Then I'm afraid that this is a missed opportunity," I force myself to reply, my own smile feeling brittle. "I am sorry. Please let the Monsignor Adams know that I will call his office as soon as I get home." The Monsignor's name is Bryant.

He doesn't notice. That's when the alarm bells really start going off. I'm already backing away from the screen when he lunges up close to it suddenly and presses his hands against the mesh. "It will only take five minutes. You should really let me in."

A cold sweat has broken out on my body, and I'm backing away to close the door even before he starts rattling at the screen door handle. Then suddenly, a huge shape looms up behind him.

"May I help you with something?" Carl rumbles in the most forbidding tone I have ever heard from him.

Roland freezes, and then turns his head, blinking slowly and mechanically. "Oh," he says in a strangely casual voice, as if a huge, intimidating neighbor was simply something he hadn't planned for.

"He says he's here from the diocese. From Monsignor *Adams*."

Carl folds his arms and stares at the man icily. "Is that so? There *is* no Monsignor Adams in New Orleans."

I can't see the man's face, but my guess is he's no longer smiling. "Oh. Well. Perhaps I'm in the wrong neighborhood." He starts to edge around Carl, who turns to watch him the entire way.

"Maybe you're in the wrong *state*, my friend. I'd rectify that quickly if I were you."

The man bobs his head as he hurries down the walk. "I'll certainly keep that in mind!"

Carl turns back to me, shaking his head. I come out and slip an arm around him for comfort as we watch the man retreat to a smallish black sedan that screams "rental." "Do you think he was a con artist or something?" I ask in a small voice as he moves his arm to wrap around me protectively.

"Or a burglar, casing the place. Or something worse." He's staring at the back of the car, and I realize after a moment that he's taking down the license plate number on his phone. "I'm gonna do a little background research on our boy, and I think we should mention this incident to the police." He winks at me. "Got a picture of him, too."

"You're the best." I nestle against him, enjoying his warmth and scent. The weather is warm enough that we don't need jackets, and I'm happily taking advantage.

He nuzzles the top of my head briefly. "Jenny's at daycare until three. Let's get this over with, and then I'll take you to lunch."

"I'd like that." I feet another glow of adoration for Carl. He had just made bringing up a date a whole lot easier. *Lucky thing, too, because I have no idea what I'm doing here.*

On the short drive over, it's all I can do not to start touching him again. I hold off so I don't distract him while he's driving, but I have to squeeze my hands between my knees like I'm worried they'll wander over to him on their own.

"Your alternatives are somewhat limited due to the lack of any physical violence," fox-faced Officer Jamie Eames tells us as we fill out the report together. "But there are other witnesses, there was an assault on an officer, and some of what your sister is charged with involves two cops, with dash cam footage to back it up. That's going to be true no matter what you choose to do.

"Disturbance of the peace, drunk driving, disorderly conduct—all those things are a slam dunk, as is filing a false police report. Cocaine and a weapon were also found in her vehicle. She's going down for those." He gives me a very direct look, and I swallow as I sit stiffly in the chair across his desk.

Next to me, Carl gives my hand a reassuring squeeze.

"How long will she go away for?" I ask, forcing myself to speak clearly. I'm shaking inside. *Once she gets out she'll hate me even more.* But maybe by then, I'll be gone.

"I'm afraid it's not that simple." The cop gives us both an apologetic smile.

"Explain," Carl replies evenly, but with a slight edge to his tone. I sit silently, my expression as calm as I can manage.

"Shayla posted bail immediately, in cash. She's a free woman until her court date, which is in three weeks."

"Three weeks?" I can't keep the panic out of my voice. Carl immediately cuts in, as if sensing that I'm at my limit.

"The potential for violence here was explained to the judge, correct? Her history of harassment and abuse?" He sounds so businesslike, in spite of standing there in his leather jacket and jeans, with his scruffy hair brushing against his collar. I wonder where he learned so much about criminal law.

There's so much about him that I just don't know. And maybe I should be afraid of that fact. After all, he might like me now, but that could change.

But I have to have faith in him. I have to believe in all that he's done, that what he says is true, and that he won't fail me when I need him most—by abandoning me, by betraying me, by being cruel...or by dying and leaving me alone.

"I'm sorry. But Judge Carhart saw the lack of violent history here, and decided that he couldn't keep her."

I drift off in my head to that dark, cold place where I once lived, where everything pretty was stolen or smashed. Where Shayla gave me misery day and night and my parents tried to patch it up with apologies, excuses, and gifts. *She can't be stopped,* I think illogically, and wonder if I'll ever be free.

Then Carl's hand wraps firm and warm around my wrist, and I turn my head to catch his fierce gaze. "Don't check out on me, sweetheart," he commands gently, and I snap back suddenly into the present.

I shudder and blink the tears out of my eyes. *He promised he would help me and protect me. Can I believe in him? Can I put my life in his hands?*

Can the two of us together do what I found so hard to do on my own?

"Okay," I mumble. "Let's talk about what options I do have."

8

CARL

"You did really well in there, sweetheart. I know it was tough to sit and listen to all that and make a decision right there. Not to mention all the extra paperwork. But believe me, starting an investigation into Shayla's abuse of you and filing an order of protection against her were both smart moves."

Emmeline sits quietly in my kitchen as I grill us up some chicken for sandwiches. She asked if we could be somewhere less public for a while, and I immediately proposed my place and lunch.

The preschool's now got Jenny until five, which she'll love because most of her friends stay until five too. That way, I can make sure Emmeline's looked after before I send her home for a nap.

"Do you do anything for your PTSD, sweetheart?" I ask very gently.

"Huh?" her head snaps around and she blinks at me as if she's worried that I just read her mind. "How did you know...?"

"Dealt with it myself for a while. You can recover, though through a lot of the process it feels like you never will." I keep my voice low and calm as I turn the chicken breasts on my hibachi and paint them with lemon, olive oil, and pulverized herbs.

"I barely know anything about you," she mumbles. "I'm scared I'll tell you things about me and you'll reject me for them."

It's the most naked confession I've ever gotten from a woman. Sweet Mary, whom I adored, hid her pain from everyone until she snapped. I'm glad as hell that Emmeline isn't doing the same. At least, not with me.

I turn down the heat, flip the chicken one last time to finish the sear, and then leave them to cook through as I walk over to take Emmeline in my arms. She gasps and slides her hands up my arms, hips tipping against mine in subtle reflex. "I have my own skeletons in my closet."

She nods, looking up at me searchingly, then murmurs, "Carl...I feel better when I'm with you. I don't mind that you're not perfect."

I flash a brief, wry grin. "Well, I don't mind that you're not perfect either, all right? Look, I'll start if you want."

It's a risk. A risk that could end with me getting thrown in jail if she spills it to the wrong people. And she might judge me. *But...here goes. If I want trust, I have to give it.*

"My uncle ran pot into America over both borders for twenty years, starting in the nineteen sixties. You could say he came back from Vietnam a changed man. He had six bullets in him that they couldn't pull out, and though he lived another forty years, he always had pain.

"This was way before medical pot, but people have been using weed as medicine for a long time. So, he ran—and smoked—a ton of it. He would give half his stuff out to other vets like him. He didn't care about the risk—he just wanted to help people.

"So eventually he retires, and I take over the plane while he handles the connections. And we make a ton of money. But then pot starts going legal all over the place.

"Uncle Jake and I decided to go legit. We poured our seed money into a legal pot farm out in Humboldt County, and settled down to become growers and producers. That's where my money came from." I shrug, wondering how awkward this is going to be. I have hinted around at it with her, but she had no idea of the scope until now.

"Wow, that's kind of a new one for me. I've never even smoked." Her voice has a nervous laugh in it, but she doesn't look angry or put off.

"Well, I can fix that any time—after Jenny's bedtime, of course. So it doesn't bother you?"

She shakes her head, smiling a little. "Not so much. You're so careful around your daughter that it doesn't exactly make me worry you're some reckless pothead who is endangering her. Besides, the local cops respect you."

"Yeah, well, they had better. That fancy new body armor they have came out of my pocket." I go back to turn the chicken again, letting it sit longer on each side now that it has seared. "So my question for you is, is the PTSD from your sister, or is it from something else?"

"A mix, probably," she admits in a soft, sad tone that gets me in the gut. "My sister made my childhood rough, and then made my adulthood even rougher after we lost our parents. But that's not why I went through so much therapy in the last year, no."

"You feel like telling me what happened?" I coax, not quite using my command tone. She has baggage, and I need to make sure it's not the kind that will cause trouble for me or for my daughter. I'll help her either way, but since I crave her in my arms so much, I need to make sure.

Then she tells me. The car bomb that took her parents—and

almost killed her, too. I hadn't made the connection between last year's explosion in the Garden District, but now I do the math.

Unstable sister. Unknown, uncaught bomber. Murdered parents. Broken faith. Now I just want to hold her so I can drown out all this crazy shit she's been dealing with.

Instead, still treading carefully, I finish fixing her lunch.

"You know, one of the priests I talked to yelled at me for giving up after I woke up in the hospital. He told me I damned myself." She sips her jasmine tea and watches me bring over the sandwiches: chicken on toasted baguette with Dijon sauce, Roma tomatoes, and lettuce.

"Priests are as likely as anyone else to be complete tools, honey. He hasn't been there. He has no idea what it's like to have someone die right in front of you, especially someone that you loved for a long time." I settle into my seat.

She looks up at me. "But you do." It's not a question.

I think of the water rushing around me as I smashed the window of Mary's sedan to free my tiny daughter from the rapidly flooding car. I managed it somehow, her coughing and crying the whole time, and got her to the rescuers on shore.

But when I went back for Mary, she fought me. She wanted to sink with that car. I have a long, faint scar on my arm, almost three years old, where she slashed it open with a twisted bit of metal to keep from being dragged free.

"Yeah," I mutter quietly. "Jenny's mother, she, uh...well, she killed herself. Drove her car off a pier with her and Jenny in it. I was right behind them. Thank God, because I managed to get Jenny out. But Mary was gone."

She gasps, and then nods, lips pressed together and her eyes brimming. "You do know, then. I'm so sorry."

"Yeah." My throat is tight suddenly, and I have to look away for a moment. "Look, whatever happens with your sister, I promise you that you're not facing it alone anymore."

She looks at me like I hung the moon, and suddenly the savory-smelling sandwiches can't keep my interest. "That means so much to me, Carl. I'm just sorry we had to meet in such bad circumstances."

"Yeah, well, better that than not meet at all." My cock aches and throbs inside my jeans, and I feel the familiar craving for her softly curving body rise up to overwhelm me again.

I don't know which of us gets up first, but we meet halfway around the table and seize hold of each other. She clings to me like a mast in a storm and offers her mouth, eyes bright and hooded. I kiss her fiercely, until she goes a little limp in my arms.

"Push my limits, please," she whispers against my mouth. "I know you'll be careful with me."

Ungh. Now I'm so turned on that I can barely see straight. "All right. But I want to hear you tell me to stop if that is what you need. If you can't speak, slap my arm three times. Do you understand me?"

There's no time to negotiate much, but I'm damned well negotiating limits and safe words. I don't play without them.

She stands there frozen. I lift an eyebrow and slide my hand from her side over the mound of her breast, finding her erect nipple through the soft green fabric. I stroke it sharply, and she gasps. "Y-yes," she answers, and I nod, satisfied.

"Then let's go upstairs." I scoop her into my arms and chuckle as she gasps again.

9

EMMELINE

I freeze up inside for a moment as he scoops me into his arms. It's something new, and a little risky, and my stomach flutters with nerves. But my choices are pretty clear: stop and stay in my comfort zone, or trust him, step out of it, and fulfill these cravings that I barely understand.

I choose the latter, and he takes me up the stairs, my heart pounding wildly as I struggle against what almost feels like stage fright. Except that instead of getting up in front of a public speaking class, I'm trying to lose my virginity—to a great guy, I might add. I can't afford to let my anxiety or inexperience get in the way.

Except...it's more than that. Shayla's voice hisses at me from my memories, darkly amused at my self-consciousness. *Once he sees the width of your ass under that skirt he's gonna throw you back down the stairs, you fat slut.*

No. Stop it. Stop. I shudder and cling to Carl harder, burying my face in his chest, feeling his heart beat strongly against my cheek. He holds me closer. He's into this.

Suddenly I get angry—really angry. My shitty sister isn't

even here and she's still messing up my life. *Fuck Shayla. She thinks any ass is huge because she doesn't have one.*

"What's up, sweetheart?" he rumbles softly in my ear as he reaches the top landing. I can hear mild concern in his voice.

"Um." I don't want to admit how nervous I am, or why. It's embarrassing. But then again...if I don't tell him, he might think it's him I have a problem with. Or sex.

"I...I've never been naked in front of anyone before," I finally admit.

He blinks down at me, and then smiles slowly. "Well, believe it or not, pretty much everybody is self-conscious about their first time, baby girl. Even me."

I stare. "Even you? But you're so...."

He laughs as he carries me down the wide, breezy hall into a master bedroom three times the size of my own. The dark, polished wood floor, beams, and furniture stand out against the pale plaster walls and ceiling. His low, broad bed is covered with a velvet coverlet of deep green.

"You think I was this confident at sixteen? Nope. You earn it, every bit of it." He carries me over to a dressing mirror next to his wardrobe and sets me gently on my feet. "Lucky for you, I'm here to help."

He leans over my shoulder from behind and kisses me, his mouth teasing mine. He lingers for only a moment before he strips off his flannel shirt and tosses it aside. I stand there facing my reflection, but watching his in the mirror.

"It's funny. I've been dreaming about seeing your body for months, but here you are shy about it and hiding in all these clothes." He runs his hands down my sides and over my hips, and I shiver at the soft pressure.

His hands seem to radiate heat as they slide over me, caressing me through my clothes. He takes my face in his hand

and gently turns my head to face my reflection. "Look," he murmurs in my ear. "Let me show you how I see you."

I look at myself in the mirror as his hands slide over me, and my gaze reluctantly trails from the path of his fingers to the body he's caressing. The body I almost concealed under a nun's habit, forever safe from scrutiny or criticism.

He reaches around me from behind and slides his hands over my shoulders. "Step out of your shoes, dear."

I do, wiggling my toes in relief. He kicks the pumps gently aside and reaches around to start slowly unbuttoning my blouse. His breath stirs the hairs on the back of my neck...and then his lips start caressing my skin.

I see my eyes widen in the mirror, and then hood. My head droops to the side, everything leaving my mind but the warm caresses of his mouth on me. His nimble fingers tug each little pearl button free of its hole; between each one he dips his fingertips into the gap in the fabric and spreads it wider.

"Now seriously, sweetheart," he purrs in my ear, "do you really see anything here that's not to like? Because I sure as hell don't."

I meet my own eyes in the mirror as he unbuttons my blouse and slides his hands inside to rub and knead my breasts. His thumb does that teasing little back-and-forth across my nipple, and I see myself smile and toss my head slightly with pleasure.

He slides the open blouse off my shoulders, and I look at the smooth skin and dark, lacy bra he reveals. I suck air in through my teeth, my nerves threatening again. I feel so vulnerable, just standing there. But then I catch the look on his face, and the feeling starts to fade.

His eyes are wide with delighted fascination, and he cups my breasts reverently, like they're treasures. When he bends to kiss my neck again, he lets out a hungry little growl that excites me more than anything he's done to my body so far. This body, which I'm familiar with to the point of contempt, but that he desires.

His hands fumble at the belt of my skirt. I hesitate, my stomach getting jumpy...and then steel myself. I shimmy my hips a little to help him pull the cloth down over them, and he grunts with pleasure as my ass bumps against his crotch. It actually makes me smile a little. *Well, guess he doesn't think my ass is too big.*

My skirt hits the floor along with my half-slip, and his hands immediately slide down to cup the cheeks of my ass and knead them firmly. "Your body is fucking amazing," he growls in my ear, "and I won't hear anything else about it."

He sets his teeth against my shoulder, nibbling his way across it and over the back of my neck. His powerful hands caress me roughly, deliciously, moving around and over my hips, up my belly, until finally he cups my breasts through the lace again and starts stroking them.

He uses the scratchy lace and the thin silk beneath artfully, teasing my nipples as I squirm and moan. His mouth runs down the top of my spine, until finally he reaches my bra clasp—and opens it with his teeth. I gasp, and then hurriedly slide the straps off my shoulders so he can pull it off me.

My gasp becomes a low moan as he tosses the bra away and starts rubbing and teasing my bare skin. Every time he touches my nipples it sends electric shocks straight down to my aching cunt. My whole body feels awakened...and full of longing I don't understand.

My hips circle reflexively as he strokes me and nibbles at my neck, bumping my ass against his crotch until he groans and starts grinding back against me. I feel his erection rub against my ass cheeks, barely caged by fabric.

My eyelashes flutter, and I'm panting and whimpering in his arms while my hands pluck impatiently at the hip straps of my panties. I wiggle out of them and kick them away into the dark.

"It feels so good," I whimper. My knees are buckling, and my eyes slide closed with pleasure. He scoops me up again and carries me to his bed. The coverlet is silky against my back and makes me tingle more as I slide onto it.

I look up to see him staring down at me fiercely as he unbuttons his jeans and shoves them down. His cock gleams like it's been polished as it springs up against his belly from a nest of golden hair. I wonder if he'll thrust into me right away—and then cry out in surprise as he lunges forward to pin me against the bed.

His cock slides against my thigh as he dives for one of my breasts instead, growling softly as he takes my nipple into his mouth. He starts to lick it in long strokes—and I shake, pressing it eagerly against his lips, wanting more.

The first hard suck forces me to muffle a scream against the nearest pillow. It's too much pleasure—so much that it almost scares me. I squirm and cry, even as my arms and legs wrap around him eagerly. I edge closer to telling him to stop with each long pull, my heart pounding so hard...

"Oh! Oh, *oh*, too much...too good," I sob, and he backs off, looking down at me as he licks his lips.

"You think you can be a good girl and take it for me?" he rumbles in a voice that makes my cunt ache even harder. "I've got a treat for you if you do."

I run my thigh against the shaft of his cock and feel him shiver. I take a deep breath. "O-okay." For him, I'd do anything.

Seconds later I have to bite back screams. He's pinning me down. His huge hands circle my wrists, his thighs pin my legs, and even though my body fights reflexively from overloaded nerves, I don't tell him to stop.

I moan and stretch against him, stunned by how good it

feels, my toes clenched and my feet sliding rhythmically against the coverlet. My legs are tangled up with him, and every now and again I feel him thrust impatiently against my thigh. His mouth is so hot that it feels like it will burn me, but I can't stop pressing my breasts against his face.

When he lets go of my wrists I can't control my hands. They're in his hair, clutching his shoulders, grabbing the coverlet. His mouth lifts away from my breast and moves to my other, while one big hand grips my whole vulva and starts kneading it. He's gentle at first, but as I rock against him insistently, he pushes harder.

My whole body burns with pleasure. I can hear my voice rising to soft yelps as tingles start to wash outward through my body with every press of his hand against my pussy. Then he pushes down harder—and holds his hand there as he starts teasing my breasts with his mouth again.

My hips rock against his palm as much as I'm able with his weight holding me down, pushing the top of my sex against him, where it aches the most for contact. My thighs part further...and then he shifts his grip and I feel something sleek and hard pressing into me.

We both gasp and shudder as he inches forward. It hurts, but only from the unfamiliarity of being stretched open. I dig my heels against the back of his calves and my fingertips into his shoulders, and push back as he sinks in deep.

"O-ohh, God," he groans, belly flexing against mine as I twine my legs around him. He holds himself still, panting and shivering as his hand keeps working my sensitive flesh. I manage to look up just once as he leans over me—and see his eyes wide open, as if he's about to start screaming himself.

I writhe and buck under him as his hips press lower and he groans through his teeth. I can't stop moving now. Something's building inside me as heat and tension gather between my thighs.

Suddenly the ache turns into bliss, blowing through my body in waves that nearly white out my mind. I let out a high sound through gritted teeth, and feel him start to thrust hard as my flesh clenches around his shaft. I push hard enough to lift him a little—and a second explosion rolls through me right on the heels of the first.

He seizes my hips and pulls me closer, pounding into me feverishly, his eyes wild, his voice growing louder and hoarser with every sharp cry he lets out.

I sob against his shoulder, overwhelmed and blissed out all at once...and then he shouts twice and lets out a long, purring groan as he stretches over me. His hips start roll slowly and sensually...and I feel a rush of warmth inside of me. He lets out a contented rumble and settles over me slowly.

He catches himself on his hands, shivering and gasping for breath. I caress his back, crooning wordlessly, and he settles his head on my shoulder. "Good girl," he whispers hoarsely.

I open my eyes from a doze a little later and find myself in his arms, the coverlet wrapped around us and my head pillowed on his bicep. "Did I prove my point?" he murmurs sleepily, nuzzling my hair.

I giggle giddily, too relaxed from satisfaction to feel self-conscious. "Yes," I murmur. "Yes, you did."

10

CARL

"What do you mean they're dropping the abuse investigation against Shayla Lacroix?" It's all I can do to keep my voice low and calm. "There are witnesses—"

"There are witnesses to just one incident, man," Jamie corrects quietly. "That's the *start* of a case. But we can't go forward until we have more." He hesitates, and the length of the hesitation as he lingers over his beer catches my attention.

I shake my head. I've spent the last two weeks caring for Emmeline, drying her post-nightmare tears and coaxing her out of her shell. The sex has been spectacular...but it's still pretty light on the spices.

Emmeline isn't going to be ready for any real kind of submission training until that bitch Shayla is out of her life for good and she's settled her head about both her abusive relationship with her sister and the murder of her parents. And the police have suddenly stopped doing their damn jobs.

"Jamie. In the past ten minutes you have told me that the investigation of Emmeline's parents' murder has been dropped due to lack of evidence, the investigation of her abuse has been dropped due to lack of evidence, and now they're calling off the investigation of the guy who showed up at Emmeline's doorstep. You want to tell me what the hell is going on?"

He tenses and glances around in an odd way. I frown and follow his gaze. He almost looks like he's worried about someone listening in. But the other patrons in this dark Irish pub are more worried about their lunchtime beers than us. "I'm not at liberty to say, which sucks."

My eyes widen as I stare at him. Jamie's solid as a rock—he's got more integrity than twenty average cops put together. And I can see the frustration lingering in his eyes. *Something stinks. And it's not my drinking buddy.*

It's New Orleans. Police brass are shorter on integrity than beat cops. By a lot.

"Let me guess." My voice lowers. "So what did Shayla use on the lieutenant—bribery, blackmail, or booty?"

"Maybe a combination," Jamie mutters, and takes a long swallow of his beer.

My jaw clenches. I've used the cops and gone through legal channels as much as I possibly can since leaving the bootlegging business. But now, it looks like "legal channels" care more about money than the law. Time to take things into my own hands.

"We can still build a case against Shayla. She's probably only going to be free a few more days. The trial's set for Thursday on her other charges." He almost sounds apologetic.

"Look, man," I break in quietly, "I know you're doing what you can. Don't overextend yourself. But if you could give me any preliminary information you were able to gather, I'll hire Molly to deal with it."

Molly Haggard is a private investigator I've used several times. She's the one that was watching Mary for me when Mary suddenly drove off for the pier with Jenny. If she hadn't warned me, Jenny wouldn't be alive, and Jamie knows it. She's back in Humboldt, but I can fly her out if needed.

He looks almost relieved. "Okay. This will take a little time, but I'll get you what I have."

At least the protection order is done, I think as I drive back home. Emmeline has mostly been staying over at my place. I've helped her unpack all her things over at hers, but as soon as my daughter is fast asleep, Emmeline is in my house and in my bed.

Jenny likes breakfasts with Emmeline. The two of them always fill my breakfast nook with bright chatter as I cook. We've had peace for a few precious days, each one starting with kisses and coffee and ending with me pinning Emmeline to whatever wall or stretch of floor or piece of furniture we haven't christened yet.

I consider it a point of pride that now that Emmeline's had a taste of real pleasure, she's always chasing it. She does it all the time, flirting with me shyly during evening cartoons. Her soft, almost sleepy gaze promises wild fucking and tenderness at the same time.

I'm falling in love with this girl, and it feels great—except for one thing. I'm about to deliver some of the worst news of her life to her, and I feel like absolute dog shit about it.

When I walk in the door, I have to stop and just...look. Emmeline's curled up on the couch napping with Jenny, who is nestled against her with her puppy in her arms. I look for a moment longer, and then smile and take a few pictures on my phone.

I'll tell her later. And meanwhile, I'll take care of this.

I go straight to my office, shut the door, and call Molly. She picks up on the third ring. "Carl. Hey, how's it going?"

"Not so good." I explain the situation in brief, hearing her type away and occasionally grunt acknowledgment as she takes notes on her laptop.

"You're right. It seems pretty suspect that 'someone' made almost every investigation involving the Lacroix family just go away. I'm actually surprised that she didn't make the other charges vanish too."

"Kind of hard to do with a dash cam recording and two bruised cops," I point out, and she grunts again.

"So you're waiting on information from Jamie?"

"I actually got it by email on my way home. I'll forward it. He didn't get very far in his investigation before they shut it down, but the bombing last year has a fifty page long file." I flip my laptop open, check my mail and start forwarding the relevant files. "With that much information they should at least have a suspect, but I couldn't find one."

"Okay, I'll start going through what we do have. Any insights on where to start other than skimming through this thing?"

"I have a photograph of a man who tried to con his way into Emmeline's house the same week that this all came to a head. He claimed to be from the diocese. I got clear shots of him and even one of his rental car's license plate."

"So start with rental car agencies." She puffs thoughtfully. "I'll see if I can draw a connection between him and any of the rest of this."

"Okay. I'll send you everything. As soon as you notice any patterns or suspicious details, let me know." I take a deep breath, closing my eyes. "I'll wire your usual retainer."

"Thanks kindly, big guy. I'll call you back soon." The connection breaks and I sit back in my chair, eyes narrowing.

"So this is what we know so far," I tell Emmeline as I hold her hands later that night. Jenny is up in her room playing with her puppy while pretending to be asleep. I'm letting her get away with it for now.

"Your parents had no enemies, no creditors, and no debtors. They had no connection to local criminal groups. They had no interests that would bring them in contact with the sort of people who generally blow up cars." I squeeze her hands gently.

I still haven't told her that the police have had their leashes yanked. She's safe, as long as I'm on watch, but I'm not sure she could deal with anymore shit from Shayla.

I'm pretty damn suspicious, though. Why would Shayla try to stop the murder investigation?

"Could it have been mistaken identity?" Emmeline asks softly. She's calmed down in the last few days, as she's learned to trust me with her safety and her life. She's grown more confident too, and I don't want to tell her anything that might set her back.

"It could have, except for one thing. They found part of the detonator. It was on a remote. Whoever killed your parents and tried to kill you was watching the whole time."

She goes so pale that I immediately shut up and pull her into my arms. "I'm sorry, baby," I murmur into her hair. "Let's take a break from talking about this for a while."

"I'm sorry," she mumbles against my neck, immediately giving me an awkward boner. "I wish I could be tougher for you."

"You're tougher than you think. You're just hurting and exhausted. And in the meanwhile, you've got me to be tough for you."

That makes her relax against me, and I smile into her hair. We might be starting slow...but every mile of the journey is going to be awesome. We just have to get rid of Shayla.

"You ever think of leaving New Orleans?" I ask quietly. "I've got all that land over in Cali. People are nice there. And Shayla would get stopped at the gate."

I haven't thought of returning to my place outside Eureka since Mary died. It hurt too much to stay. Instead, we moved to be close to Mary's mother, since she had no one left to help her get through.

I love New Orleans, and we have ties here now. But if Emmeline says the word, I'll pick up and move across the country in a heartbeat. Anything to make her feel safer.

"This is my home," she says simply. "I know that it has its problems, and that Shayla is here. But no, I've never considered leaving."

I nod again and hold her close. "Then we stay." *And make a stand.*

Unfortunately, until Molly comes back with something substantial, we're stuck waiting for Shayla to make a move.

It doesn't take her long. It's two days later when she makes her move, and it nearly blinds me with rage.

"What happened?" Emmeline asks in a light panic as I throw on my leather jacket. "Is Jenny all right?"

"She's fine. The daycare staff refused Shayla entry. They sure as hell didn't let her take Jenny home with her, no matter how much she insisted that she's my girlfriend." *I'm going to kill that bitch.*

"I'm so sorry," she starts, and I turn back to her.

"Don't do that, sweetheart. This is not your fault. You stay here and keep the shades drawn, the lights off, and everything locked up. If anyone approaches the house that you don't know, you call me at once. Okay?"

She nods. "Okay."

My phone rings as I stalk outside and walk to my truck, which is parked down the street while I repair my driveway. It's Molly. I almost don't pick up.

"Bad timing. Shayla tried to grab my kid from her daycare. I'm on my way over there."

I start walking past the steel dumpsters out front that hold the stained and crumbling old blacktop, digging out my keys. But then Molly asks something that slows my walk.

"Wait. Did Shayla have any hope of actually getting in?"

"No, daycares don't hand kids off to just any strange adult. I'm actually surprised Shayla didn't know that."

"She did. Don't go. It's a diversion!" Her voice has an actual edge of panic to it.

"Wait. How do you know?" I stop short. I'm almost to my truck, but the fear in her voice bothers me.

"That car you photographed was rented by Shayla, in cash. It was the second time she rented from that agency, which is by the airport. You said this Roland guy is probably from out of town?"

"Yeah." My eyes narrow. "The local Monsignor's always in the news, but he didn't even know the guy's name. He also had an accent, and no tan."

"I think Shayla flies this guy in to do her dirty work when she wants someone dead. Like whoever is between her and half a billion dollars' worth of inheritance money." She takes a deep breath. "Like her own parents."

"Or Emmeline." I turn around in a desperate hurry. "I'll call you back."

I take one step back beside the dumpsters—and my truck goes up in a fireball behind me.

11

EMMELINE

I hear myself scream as the explosion shakes the windows. I burst out the door, see Carl's truck in flames...and everything goes gray and distant.

I sit down on the front steps, staring at the fireball. *Carl.* My world has just blown up again...and this time, it's not just my world. How will I tell Jenny?

I can't move. I'm too cold. When a figure in white steps out of a van parked across the street, opens the gate and strolls up to me, I can't even lift my head.

He ducks down instead, and I see Roland's lopsided smile. "Hi there," he says cheerily. "Looks like you've got a problem with keeping loved ones."

He grabs me by the arm and yanks me to my feet just as Shayla pulls up in her gold Mercedes. She smirks as she sees the fire. "Good work, my little errand boy," she says archly.

Roland shoots her an annoyed look. "Don't call me that," he warns, but she just laughs and stalks past me into Carl's house.

"Bring her inside. I want to have some fun."

I'm too numb to do anything as they half-drag me into the dining room. The next thing I know, I'm tied to one of the dining room chairs, but I don't know how exactly I got there, my mind and body slowly having given up on me. Then Shayla leans into my face and smirks at me. "So, you're gonna die. You should have given up that money when you had the chance, sweetie. Mama needs a new pair of shoes."

I just stare at her, barely comprehending what she's saying. Carl's gone. He was supposed to be the one to protect me, and instead...I'll be burying him too. And it's all because of Shayla.

I feel a faint ember of anger and hate under all the weight of my despair, but it's not enough yet to make me shake it off and do something. I hate this world. I can't deal with any of this.

But then I think of Jenny, and how she's going to be left alone after this—just like I was. And how Shayla and her...friend...have gotten away with everything.

The ember grows into a spark. The gray fog starts to clear a little. *I need to think. What do I do?*

I let them tie me to the chair, but I can hear, and I can speak. I hold off on the second, letting Shayla yammer on.

"You know, none of this would have happened if you hadn't gone back for your phone that afternoon. Really, honey, you're completely useless. Why couldn't you have just died with Mom and Dad when Roland blew their car?" Her mocking croon scrapes against my ears...and I feel my anger grow.

"You?" I ask, pretending it takes more effort than it does.

She laughs. "Yeah! Me! You think I'm waiting around until I have gray hair to get what's coming to me? I want to be a billionaire now, while I'm young and hot!"

I stare at her as Roland moves back and forth in the room behind me. I hear sloshing and smell gasoline. *Oh shit. This man means to kill me, just like he did my parents. Only my death will be...slower.*

Time for me to unleash my secret weapon. The one thing she can't handle, which has grown stronger in me since Carl showed me what love and protection can be like. "You sure you don't just owe your coke dealer?"

Her jaw drops, and Roland bursts into soft laughter. She shoots him a glare. "Shut up and keep working!"

"I am a professional assassin, not your pet goon." There's an edge to his voice. "Lend a hand if you want the place in flames faster."

"I don't do manual labor! I'm the one paying you!" Shayla sniffs and turns back to me. "I'm going to untie one of your hands and put Dad's straight razor in it. Then I'm going to set the room on fire. You've got two choices. Take your own life quickly, or burn."

"Are we certain that we want to give her a weapon?" Roland doesn't sound too impressed with her dastardly plan.

"Shut up! This is my show. You're just the help."

"This is how she talks to everyone," I pipe up. "I'm her blood sister and she wants to burn me to death. She had her own parents blown up for money. You think she'll treat you with respect?"

Roland snorts. "None of *you* would kill her for disrespecting you."

Shayla backs off of me and stomps over to confront Roland. "Kill me? You're gonna kill *me*? Who the fuck is going to pay for your plane tickets and fancy hotels if you start gunning down your clients?"

I look down at my wrists, which are still tied to the arms of the chair. I was so limp that they barely bothered to tie me securely. *Carl's tied me tighter than this.* I start rocking my wrists back and forth, trying to get a little play in the rope so I can draw my hands out.

The two of them are bickering now instead of paying attention to me. "No one's going to tie me to any of the deaths around here," Roland sneers as I quietly struggle. "So watch your step."

"You watch your step!" Shayla's madness and ego have taken over, and she doesn't see the way his eyes are narrowing as he stares at her. "I could buy you! I could buy ten of you!"

"Can you buy yourself a proper ass?" he sneers.

"Nope," I add helpfully. This is actually a little bit fun—especially since I'm no longer all that scared of what will happen to me.

I just know one thing: I am not letting them burn down Carl's house with Jenny's puppy hiding somewhere in here. I will not let them take a single thing more away from anyone...even if that means making them stop each other.

Roland snickers again. "Honestly, I like her better than you. She's not a psychotic twat who doesn't know when to shut her mouth."

"Yes she is. Your little bombing job left her with PTSD. For a while we thought she was going to the nut house instead of a nunnery."

Roland stops dead. "Wait, wait. She was actually going to be a *nun*? Vows of poverty, all of that? She would have gotten out of the way without us doing anything, and you would have inherited your parents' money as soon as they died of natural causes?"

Angry tears fill my eyes. "Yes."

He turns to me, staring. "You would have gone and become a holy woman." For a moment there's a twitch of...something...in the back of those empty eyes.

"Yeah. I was about to start serving as a novice."

Puzzlement fills his expression. "What happened?"

I explode suddenly, pulling against the ropes so hard that the chair arms creak. "*You* happened! You and that crazy bitch over there! You killed my parents and you tried to kill me!"

This isn't manipulation. I'm not just talking back to drive my sister off-balance and make her argue with a dangerous assassin. This is raw emotion pouring out of me.

"How in the hell can I believe in God when this psycho ruined my childhood, tried to ruin my life, and is now trying to burn me alive? How can I believe in any kind of divine justice when murderers like you and her are allowed to just walk around free? How?"

"How indeed?" muses a deep voice from the hallway behind Roland.

Shayla's jaw drops and she just turns and stands there, peering down the hall toward the back door like she's seen a ghost. I hear the sound of a shotgun cocking.

Roland moves like lightning, his lean white form darting behind the nearest cover as he draws a gilded pistol from beneath his suit coat. Unfortunately for Shayla, the nearest cover is her. He grabs her and yanks her backwards against him as a human shield, holding the pistol over her shoulder.

"You'll hit your lover's sister," he taunts the unseen figure with the raspy voice. I feel very dizzy suddenly.

"I'll hit my lover's abuser. Drop the gun. Or I'll blow you both away."

Carl?

"Um..." Roland looks between the hallway and me, and then glances back at the door behind me. "I don't think you'll do that in cold blood."

"Bitch, you splashed gasoline all over my kitchen and living room! Nobody's going to believe this isn't self-defense!"

Roland blinks once—and then shrugs. "Goodbye."

He shoves Shayla forward and yanks the front door open, bursting out onto the porch. I can hear running feet—and then the yelp of sirens as at least one cruiser pulls up. *Guess the fire caught too much attention for even the lieutenant to brush off.*

Shayla is on her ass, trying to get to her feet in stiletto heels. They skid on the hardwood as she stares up at whoever is walking slowly down the hall toward her. "I had you killed!" she complains.

"Yeah." Carl coughs as he steps into view in the doorway, his voice raspy. His clothes are torn, muddy, and full of hedge leaves. His face is bloodied, and he looks plenty pissed off...but he is very much alive. "Well, you did a piss poor job of it."

He turns his shining smile on me. "Hi baby. Told you I'd protect you."

I smile through my tears. "Yes. You did."

In the end, all Shayla could do once she ranted off empty threats was sit on the floor and cry like an overwrought toddler. I watched her while Carl untied me with blistered hands, and wondered why I had ever feared her—before she hired an assassin, at least.

The police brass seemed to understand that they had a mess on their hands, and the lieutenant who had taken Shayla's bribe was quietly fired. Shayla and her errand boy were packed off to jail.

Carl took Jenny, Flubber, and I off to vacation in Humboldt for a few weeks while the lawyers sorted out the redistribution of my parents' estate. I saw sea lions for the first time, and drank California wine.

He introduced me to ball gags, so that I could scream as much as I wanted even with Jenny sleeping in the next room. (They're getting a lot of use).

I hired a cleaning crew for my parents' house and someone to redecorate, and someone to sell off my sister's things while we were in California. I kept myself busy by day. Carl kept me busy by night.

By the time we pull up in front of my family home in the Garden District, other than the permanent burn scar on one of the trees, there's no trace of Shayla left in this place at all. I have even had her room repainted. And I made sure the yard was safe—and escape-proof—for both dogs and little kids.

I smile proudly as the stately old house looms before us, and Jenny gasps with joy. "It's a castle!" she cries. "Look, Daddy, I told you Emmie's a princess! She lives in a castle!"

He laughs and tightens his grip on me, kissing my temple. "I already knew that, sweetie. Anyway, now you live in a castle too. This is our new home."

Her face lights up even more. "Come on, Flubber!" she calls, and the wandering puppy barks and scrambles after her as she hurries up the stairs to the door. "We're gonna live here!"

"So how did you get everything ready for us?" Carl's voice is still a little raspy, but his throat has healed. We walk up the stairs more slowly, arm in arm.

"Oh, you know. Deep cleaning, a premature estate sale."

"No exorcism?"

I think of Shayla, now sulking in a cell. "We already handled that."

He laughs and wraps an arm around me as we go to join his daughter. "That we did."

The End.

SIGN UP TO RECEIVE FREE BOOKS

S ign Up to Receive Free E-Books and Audiobook Codes.

Would you like to read **Savage Hearts** and **other romance books** for **free?**

You can sign up to receive free e-books and audiobooks by typing this link into your browser:

https://ivywondersauthor.com/ivy-wonders-author

©Copyright 2020 by Michelle Love & Eliza Duke - All rights Reserved

In no way is it legal to reproduce, duplicate, or transmit any part of this document in either electronic means or in printed format. Recording of this publication is strictly prohibited and any storage of this document is not allowed unless with written permission from the publisher. All rights are reserved.

Respective authors own all copyrights not held by the publisher.

❦ Created with Vellum

www.ingramcontent.com/pod-product-compliance
Lightning Source LLC
LaVergne TN
LVHW011733060526
838200LV00051B/3170